Ré Ó Laighléis is a writer of adult and teenage fiction in both English and Irish. His novels and short stories have been widely translated into various languages and he has been the recipient of many literary awards, including Bisto Book of the Year awards, Oireachtas awards, the North American NAMLLA Award and a European White Ravens Award. In 1998, he was presented with the 'An Peann faoi Bhláth' award by the President of Ireland, Mary McAleese, in recognition of his contribution to Irish literature. He is a former Writer-in-Residence at the National University of Ireland, Galway (2001) and held the same post with Mayo County Council in 1999.

A Dubliner by birth, he was reared in Sallynoggin and, since leaving teaching in Galway in 1992, has lived in the Burren, Co. Clare.

By the same author

The Great Book of the Shapers

A right kick up in the Arts

Ré Ó Laighléis

MÓINÍN

Published by MÓINÍN
Ballyvaughan, Co. Clare, Ireland
E-mail: moinin@eircom.net

First print 2006

A CIP catalogue record for this book is available
from the British Library.

ISBN 0-9532777-8-X

Set in Palatino 10.5/14pt

Lines from 'April, come she will'. Copyright © 1965 Paul Simon.
Used by permission of the Publisher: Paul Simon Music.

Cover design by Raydesign

Typeset and design by Carole Devaney

Printed in Ireland by Clódóirí Lurgan, Indreabhán, Co. Galway

Foreword

The *Shaper* relates specifically to the world of the Arts as does the *poseur* to the world in general. He or she is an animal of its own making, incestuous and parasitical in nature, and intent only on perpetuating its own existence. The shaper is the bane of the life of the true artist and arts administrator, latching on to either or both and convincing him or herself that art, in any form, simply cannot exist without him / her.

The shaper is the writer of many books or plays, the composer of many works of music, the painter of amazing profiles and landscapes, and the organiser of multiple events, none of which ever have reached or will reach the eyes or ears of those who might appreciate them – and this, not because the shaper deems them unworthy of display before a wider audience, but because, at best, these works / events are, and have been from the outset, nothing more than figments of the shaper's imagination. A prolonged adolescence, sometimes running into its fifties and, indeed, sixties, has enabled the shaper justify his or her existence simply by the claim of having been successful in existing. If art in any way relates to the shaper, it can only be insofar as he or she has made an artform of pretence.

The Fly

To Paul Carter, Sinéad Collins,
Alanna Corballis, Carole Devaney,
Úna Fitzgerald, Ben Gibney,
Josephine Lawless,
Tomás Mac Con Iomaire,
Tony McFadden and
Austin Vaughan –
all of whom encouraged generously
and laughed heartily
at this work as it took
– dare I say it –
shape.

1
Birth and Awakening

The sun burns hard against the mist that envelops the western hinterland of Slagway. Beyond the dewy blanket, the ocean dances, resplendent under Apollo's smile. Within, the town of Slagway sleeps, just as it has slept – for years, for decades, for centuries, indeed – until now.

A blast, as though of music – or if not that, at least of an assemblage of discordant notes, strung together by one who claims to own an instrument, or to know someone who owns an instrument, or, at the very least, indeed, to know someone who knows someone who thinks he may, one time, have seen someone carry what he thought to be an instrument – even someone else's instrument – escapes. Playing it! Well, that is another matter. Perhaps, when all is said and done, it was just … the Wind, the mystical Sirocco; the … hot air!

And on the wind, the spores. Spores! Spores stir silently and stealthily throughout the sleeping townland, readying for the off, once the time has come. They and sperm are the genitors of what will happen: the shapers of all things. And so, it is appropriate that, ever after, their product will be known amongst the common Rabble as *shaper*. This shaper will be born of all that is creative (wink-wink), of all that is artistic (double wink-wink). Such being the case, the richness, the elitist air of the more classical appellation seems better suited to such (noble!) progeny.

A search, much publicised (of course), is made amongst the early Christian documents of monastic monks. It is important that the proper term be sourced, or, to be more accurate, it is important that the Rabble be given to understand that the proper term has been sourced. Their sheepish little minds will never know to the differ. After all, as Aristotle, in his undoubted wisdom, said, '*Sí rufasta aid a loofáil*'.*

Eureka! (Bejay, did he say that one too? Or was that his brother, Archimedes? Brother!!?) Somewhere – within the town's own walls, of course; it wouldn't do if it were somewhere else – the term, in all its purity, has been sourced. Found on ancient, parched vellum – much more parched than has ever before been found in the history of the world, like, ya know. Anywhere! It has to be, you see, for this vellum has been found within the ancient walls of Slagway. And there, one whole page is given to the term, the classical term, the real term (or so the Rabble will be told). If there is any doubt about the term, the page *can, may* – not *will*, mind you – be made available for inspection … for a consideration, naturally. These things take – though they hate to mention the filthy common term – *MONEY*. MONEY, MONEY, MONEY, MONEY, MONEY. There, they've said it, and many times, purging their systems of the bastard term, then quietly fleshing (or is that flushing?) out its repulsive aura by adding 'MAKES OUR WORLD GO AROUND' … several times over.

However, lest digression thwart the announcement of the term, it is now to be definitively declared: *SHAPERUS*.

* 'They are easily fooled'.

Yes, SHAPERUS. This is it in its purest, most classical, most original (note, not just original, but *most* original) form. Texts are scanned: Longman's, Shortman's, Middleman's, Isle of Man's, Handyman's, Everyman's, and all above the level of the Rabble are agreed that SHAPERI will constitute its plural form.

SHAPERUS – SHAPERI

Shaperus	*Shaperi*
Shapere	*Shaperi*
Shaperum	*Shaperos*
Shaperi	*Shaperorum*
Shapero	*Shaperis*
Shapero	*Shaperis*

And this, forever after, will be the *shaper* in all his shapes and forms.

Rejoice then! Rejoice! A fanfare of trumpets; a roll of drums; a frenzied rubbing together of furtive hands and a secretive counting of notes … musical notes, ensues.

Notes and drum rolls, friction and more notes – rolls of notes – dissipate the mist and now Apollo, unbeknownst to the Rabble, smiles on the sleeping town of Slagway. Here and there, within the town, a spore or sperm stirs a little and a *shaperus* or two scratches his or her (no sexism here!) arsus magnus, where a common Rabble-type pimple has dared to flaw its pulchritude.

A fly, buzzing busily about the room, stirs Administratus from his sleep.

"Shite and onions," Administratus says, half-conscious in his morning state that a copy of *Ulysses*, or an abbreviated version of same, lies somewhere by the bed. Thus the would-be Joycean reader greets the Slagway morning and another day begins.

"Howaya, Martineen?"

"Howaya me arse!"

2
The Meeting of the Shapers

"Arrder, Arrder now, plase! Would the matin' plase come to arrder."

The shaperi ignore the pleas of Shaperus Secundus. The rolling of his Rs is not, as later we shall see, of the calibre of others who have gathered at the meeting. His speech has been, most sadly, polluted by a knowledge of some bastard native tongue which has served him poorly since encountering the more sophisticated shaperi who have been spawned by Slagway's upsurge in the Arse – eh, Arts! Nonetheless, there is some belief amongst those more polished in the gathering, despite his crude demeanour, his inability to articulate and enunciate with anything approaching the level of a more presentable shaperus, that Shaperus Secundus compensates considerably in his capacity as workhorse.

"Ah now, fellah shapers, let's have a bitteen of arrder, can ye! Arrder now, plase!"

They still ignore him. He looks to Shaperus Maximus, who is seated to his right. The creeping grey of Maximus' beard speaks of wisdom, of ability to handle, to master, to manipulate the crowd – even a crowd of such undoubted shaperi. Maximus can see the helplessness in the eyes of Shaperus Secundus.

"Awdawwwr, Awdawwwr," says Maximus. His ability to lengthen the terminal R and yet, artistically avoid rolling it, gains immediate attention. The shapers have quietened, fully, so quiet now that a hitherto unnoticed fly is heard to land upon the wall. All eyes look at it – the bug. Their timing is remarkable. Then, all eyes back to Shaperus Maximus, who awaits their gaze and who then nods to Shaperus Secundus. Maximus' and Secundus' eyes fix on one another, the latter honoured to be second in command, the former knowing, secretly, that if, in time, the question of succession does arise, Secundus will, of necessity, remain very much … secundus. They smile, then break their stare.

"Now, den, now dat I've managed to git year attinshun, I'd like ta git sshtarted. Der's a fair ould aginda to be got tru," Secundus says. "Have ye all got year copy of d'aginda?"

Shapers in the gathering are seen to translate the question for others who are seated around them and a belated communal 'yes' is sent back to the chair.

"Rightso, now let's git tru dis one fairly fassht. None o' d'ould shitehawkin' dat wint on lassht year, right!" says Shaperus Secundus. It is his way of encouraging the assembly. "Firssht on d'aginda is d'attindince."

He lifts the light green sheet of paper which, earlier, had passed amongst the shaperi and upon which, now, the names of all those in attendance are clearly registered. He reads silently to himself at first, perusing carefully, marking in his mind the whos and wheres of the various what whats that may arise. The roll call:

"Shaperus Maximus," he calls aloud now. "Shaperus Secundus – fé méin, meself," he says. "Shaperus Administratus" – he scans the gathering to locate the pimple-arsed Administratus, who, increasingly nowadays, is also known as 'Y-J'. "Shaperus Dramatus" – he sees him towards the back. "Shaperus Oratus" – yes, he's there too. "Shaperus Magnus," and so on and so on, litanising latinly the various other shaperi – magni, mini and musicalli medii – who have gathered in together to shape the future Annus of the Arts for Slagway. All present, with the exception of one or two who are not yet quite sure about themselves, are definitely agreed that they are there!

"I prepiss that we are all here," Dramatus says.

Secundus seconds the prepissal. He is a master of seconding and, unbeknownst to himself, very much a secondary master. He writes it down: 'Prepissed, seconded and anonymously (!!) pissed.'

"Nexssht item on d'aginda," says Secundus. He is motoring now: Item One is gone. He announces Item Two – 'The Arts in the Year Ahead' – introduces the non-needing-of-introduction Administratus and invites him to inform the gathered shaperi of the planned readings for the year ahead.

Even as he is sitting, Administratus is the height of many an upstanding man. He stands – and now he is a giant: an upstanding giant of the Arts. His voice is so unaffectedly deep that, as he clears his throat, the sound is almost unnoticed.

"Good eveninkk," he starts. "Though it iss unlikely that I am unknown to any prresent herre this eveninkk, I will, shall and / orr, indeed, should, perrhaps, forr purrposes of fforrmality, introduce myself." He looks around him, boosted by the knowledge that the clearing of his throat and the excellence of his eloquent delivery has captured them already.

"I-I-I-I am Administrratus – Shaperrus Administrratus, to be prrecise. Indeed, some of you acquainted with events morre rrecently orrganised by me may also know me as Y-J." Some nodding assertions in the gathering confirm the wisdom of his decision to announce himself in multiple appellations.

"I will prroceed to delineate forr you the majorr rreadinks orrganised by me forr the upcoming Arrts prrogrramme."

Administratus proceeds to do so. Regularly, throughout his speech, he announces as the redoubtable jewel in the crown of the upcoming readings, that which will take place some two weeks hence. He concludes with the urging that, "Iff you arre to miss any of thiss yearr's rreadinks, my frriends, let it nott be that which will be held on this night fforrtnight."

Administratus sits. Applause. He has done well. He knows he has done well. His presentation has been top class; his eloquence *par excellence*. He feels that he can read in Shaperus Maximus' face the faint and subtle signs of that approval which he so craves. Could we, some time in the future, be talking 'succession' here, he wonders.

Other speeches follow. Shapers in the different artforms delineate their programmes also. Administratus is, however, oblivious to it all. His presentation has been made and he is busy playing its better parts over and over again in his artistic mind. Administratus reattunes his mind just in time to hear Secundus finish off his presentation on the theme of this year's big parade. "In years passht, we've done tings like 'Lugliver', 'Granny Wails', 'The Boa's Bark' and dat wan about d'ould Cull o' Booley – ay, the Tawn, is it? Ay, and many many udders, all too numberous ta minshun. But dis year we're goin' ta go the whole hogg, pull out all the sshtops, be raley imagina... imagina... imag... ah, feck it – darin' like, ya know."

The shaperi are on the edges of their seats, those who have managed to simultaneously decipher what it is Secundus is saying, eagerly awaiting the announcement of this year's theme. Others, less attuned to the *subtleties* of Secundus' linguistic mix, are in arrears in the understanding stakes and are in danger of missing the announcement when it is made.

"The Fresh Air," Secundus now announces.

There is silence – silence feeding into silence and beyond. A Great Silence. Had one but the ability, and were it not for the fact that the title had been used before, one might, could, would, (but, alas, now won't) write a book about this 'Great Silence'.

"Brilliant!" a shaperus minus (*Plantus*) somewhere to the rear of the gathering is heard to whisper. Secundus, unnoticed by the others, winks in his direction.

"Brilliant!" says another of the shaperi mini (also of the genus *Plantus*).

Suddenly, a chain of 'brilliants' has linked its way throughout the assembly and 'brilliant' is the only word on the ovine lips of all. Even shapers who had failed to successfully negotiate the idiosyncrasies of Secundus' delivery are chanting 'brilliant' at this point.

Secundus raises his arms, feigning a desire that the meeting quieten now. He is secretly disappointed when, quite quickly, they respond to his gesture by acceding to the request.

"Now, den," he says, "more detail on the Fresh Air Teme as tings develop over the nexssht couple a' monts."

He waits, half hoping for some clamour for details there and then. No clamour comes.

"Right so, dat's it den, is it?" No answer. "Dat's it so, right den!" he exclaims, thinking that perhaps his innovative rearrangement of his previous question might spark a response. Still no answer. He rummages through the pages spread before him on the table. He had not expected to be referring to the agenda so soon again.

"Now den," he says, "nexssht item: The Rabble."

There is the grumble of discontent throughout the hall. A not-important shaperus stands to state assertively that this item has been on the agenda year in, year out and, as of yet, there is no discernible improvement to be seen. Mutterings of approval all round assure him that, as he sits, he has been seen, has made an impression and, all in all, is sitting down again a less unimportant shaperus than before.

Now, a somewhat more important shaperus – one Solicitoratus – stands to address the meeting:

"Well, I, being a shaperus of, though I myself do say so, not insignificant standing and with an ancestry – and, Please God, a progeny yet to come – in shaperism which has served and will serve the town of Slagway well and being, as I am, a sitting member of no less than 243 of the 245 sub-committees of shaperi, not to mention my longtime acknowledged participation in the furtherance of the Arts for those who matter, feel it should be sorted out for once and for all." The mouths of all around him are agape.

"Summararily then, I feel it should be sorted out," he

adds, quite humbly.

"Eh, tank ya, fellah shaper," Secundus says, somewhat hesitantly.

And now, a third, a woman, known to many in the hall as she who heads up the occasionally non-hibernating Poetry sub-committee, stands.

"Yes, Poetica," Secundus invites, as he sees her robust bosom rise.

"Dear Secundus, I'd like to say,
Regarding the Rabble of sweet Slagway,
We have a place for them to stay –
'Tis beyond the walls, out in the Bay.

But, lest we be hasty, let me *assay*   [poetic licence]
That before we urge them *away* to *stay*
                              [internal as well as external rhyme!]
We fleece them first and make them pay
For our sweet Arts in dear Slagway."

Devastating stuff!!!! Silence. Silence born of the excellence of such poetry! Spontaneous applause. Applause that's growing now on its own spontaneity. Rapturous. Silence once again.

"Well said, well said, Poetica – anudder jewel. Rale pottery, huh!" Secundus exclaims, winking, knowing that, in having given her her chance to speak and in following it with these words of praise, he has, at least, doubled his chance of having his way with her some time in the not too distant future.

Though others rise to contribute to the discussion, it is generally agreed that Poetica has most eloquently encapsulated the sentiment of the meeting in her contribution and that anything that is said thereafter quite simply pales by comparison. All are agreed that a sub-committee should be set up to look into this persistent problem of the Rabble.

Nominations are sought to head up the new sub-committee. Poetica, though, of course, she would "*simply love to*", cannot oblige. She is eager this year, she explains, to complete the ten-poem collection on which she has been working this past twelve years or so. She has only nine more poems to go, she tells them. Her consolation to the disappointed attendance is that it will be a work well worth waiting for ... and waiting for ... and waiting for ...

No other nominations. Now volunteers are sought. A fit of communal coughing is followed by an inexplicable, coincidental need for many in attendance to make for the double door exit towards the back end of the hall. The rush is halted and then miraculously reversed by the timely announcement by our friend, Solicitoratus – he who is so conscious of his ancestry and progeny – that "I, despite the demands of the other 243 sub-committees, 242 of which I chair, and, for the cause of safeguarding the Arts against the Rabble, thereby perpetuating the illustrious tradition which has already secured for Slagway a place in history in the annals of artistic endeavour, am prepared to chair this new and most important sub-committee."

Secundus' eyes have spiralled towards the Twilight Zone as he listens to the elegance of such verbosity. Communal coughing is now replaced by a communal '*Phew*'. Back-slapping, fair play to yas and general appreciation of this, another gobshite born (or even reborn), is expressed by one and all.

Secundus beams at the table at the top of the hall. All the signs are that his exhortation at the start of the meeting that there be no shitehawkin' this year is being heeded and is having the desired effect of getting them quickly through the agenda. It will be left to the Chairman of the new sub-committee on the Rabble to flesh out his own committee, thus saving time at this evening's meeting.

"Right so, fellah shaperi, dat laves jussht two pacific items: Firsshtly d'elecshun of d'officers and den d'address of Shaperus Maximus. D'elecshun of d'officers firssht so," Secundus says.

The coughing in the gathering is starting up again and the need of many to seek out the air for a second time is mounting when, yet another saving suggestion comes from the back of the hall. Once again, it is the shaperus minus who earlier had responded to the announcement of Secundus' Fresh Air Theme as being 'brilliant'.

"I propose that the existing committee be re-elected en masse," the shaperus minus suggests.

Secundus is struggling at the table to interpret the proposal. Jaysus, this feckin' shaperus minus is losin' the run of himself, he thinks. Give 'im a bloody inch is right!

"Re-elected en what is it?"

"En masse, Secundus, en masse," exclaims the lesser shaper. "All of them, like, ya know," he adds.

"Arragh, the lot of dem in one go, is it! Well, why, in da name of Jaysus, didn't ya say so in the firssht place!" says Secundus, "and not be ballsin' us about wit dem ould German terms of yers."

Secundus looks across at Maximus, lifts his eyes

towards the ceiling, suggesting his frustration with this irritating shaperus minus. Maximus remains quite stoic, showing neither approval nor disapproval of either minus or Secundus. Secretly, to him, they are both of a kindred nature. Secundus addresses the gathering of shapers once again.

"Right den, all dem in favour of re-electionin' the whole damn shabang *in a mess* agin, raise year right hands."

The hands, every hand (every right hand, even) in the hall is raised before Secundus finishes his instruction. "Right so! I don't tink der's any doubt about dat den. I declare the whole committee anonymously re-elected."

"Anonymously," he re-emphasises, lest there be any doubt about what it is that he has said, then adds: "And I'd like ta take dis opportunity to coagulate dem on dare re-elecshun." Secundus sits, allowing for applause.

A pause. Applause. 'Plausive applause peals pleasantly about the hall', thinks Poetica in what will, in times to come, she *muses*, be remembered as one of her more inspired alliterative moments: an example par excellence of her own '*P Period in Poesy*' ... Now there's a title deserving of a book, she thinks!

Now Secundus stands again. He has convinced himself that part of this applause is meant for him. End of applause.

"Now den, fellah shapers, if ya would plase, would ya put year hands togedder and kindly welcome Shaperus Maximus to the podi... to the podi... Arragh, would ya plase welcome Shaperus Maximus."

Now, more applause. Maximus rises, then slowly moves towards the podium, ignoring Secundus' hand, which has been extended in official welcome. He stands now, chest high above the slanted lectern, his silver strands of hair glistening beneath the fluorescence of the lighting which smiles down upon him. Somewhere amidst the gathering, a high-pitched female sigh is heard: it is Poetica, overcome by weakness at the very sight of the greatest shaper of them all, now in his upright state. Maximus is oblivious to the mini commotion caused by poor Poetica's pallid pigmentation (*Pigmentum pallidum [p]alliteratum*).

With his square and ring-bedecked forefinger, Maximus eases his bifocals from tip of nose to bridge, clears his throat and then begins ...

3
Maximus' Address:
The Announcement of the FART

"Illustrious Shapers," Maximus begins. He is immediately interrupted by an outburst of spontaneous applause and a mature and practiced stamping of shaperly feet against the wooden floor. The Fly, that winged wizard which earlier had perched itself upon the wall, is the only living creature within the town of Slagway privy to the fact that even exiled shapers, in far-flung cities in all corners of the world, across the mighty ocean to the west of this ancient city's doorstep, have been plunged onto their feet on hearing Maximus' words reverberate throughout all lands.

Things quieten again along the *Western Front* and Maximus can speak once more.

"It is fully one whole year since last I stood to deliver my address. Many of the faces I see before me now are those of esteemed shapers whom I have seen year in, year out, who have come to listen in weather fair and foul, who have been relentless in their pursuit of that holy grail which we know to be the Arts. In the presence of such shapers, one cannot but feel humbled."

The heads of those to whom he has alluded are seen to swell. In cases where any two such shapers are seated alongside each other, their respective swelling causes their ears to touch. Indeed, in rows where there are several such pairs, the level of congestion occasioned by their swelling causes some lesser shapers to leave their seats and to stand out in the side aisles. Shaperus Administratus, seeing this, makes a mental note that he must enquire of the town's Fire Chief – one of their own (i.e. Shaperus Arsonus) as to the degree of insurance cover for such sideliners. It is not, in his thinking, beyond the bounds of possibility that swelling in such numbers (particularly of ears) could lead to friction, thereby leading on to fire. Administratus believes that, in years to come, he will be thanked for his sharpness of observation in this matter and it is, indeed, an observation which can be discreetly made to reach the ears of Maximus. Oh yes, our Y-J thinks to himself, when it come to fire, Arsonus is your only man. But back to Maximus ...

"There are the faces too of others whom I do not fully recognise, but who, I'm sure, in future years, I will come to know, have they but the dedication and perseverance of their more senior brothers and sisters in the art of Shapery. Let me assure such neophytes that the day will come when their ears too will swell with praise, when, in years ahead, I stand to address the Meeting of the Shapers."

Again, there is applause and those newer shapers who had been self-damned to the aisles squeeze themselves back onto the chairs at the end of each row. There is room for all, now that the seasoned shapers earlobes have contracted once again.

"The past year, my fellow-Shapers, has not been easy on the Arse – eh, Arts," continues Maximus. His faux pas somehow registers in Y-J's subconscious and occasions him to slightly raise his lesser cheek off the chair and to discreetly scratch that irritant which has inveigled space upon his fleshy buttock.

"There has been the perennial question of venues," continues Maximus. "An ever increasing number of shapers in our town's population and yet, so very few venues to accommodate their genius." The shapers nod to one another, acknowledging their dilemma and, more particularly, their genius.

"Then there is the continuing and tortuous problem of the Rabble. It is not an issue on which I intend to dwell and, indeed, it heartens me to see here tonight that a sub-committee has been formed to deal with that matter. However, as leader of the shapers, it would be grossly remiss of me were I to let this opportunity pass without alerting you, my fellow-Shapers, against the ever-increasing danger of the common Rabble gaining access to our Arts. We must be vigilant in our defence of what is ours and ours alone. No one who is not a genuine and bona fide shaper must be allowed to meddle with the sacred and precious tradition that is the Arts."

The crowd stands now and this time the applause is deafening. A low drone wends its way from the back of the hall and very soon every shaperus lends his voice to it, transforming what was, at first, a modest incantation, into tumultuous adulation. "Maximus, Maximus, Maximus, Maximus, Maximus, Maximus," they chant. Maximus stands back from the podium and allows his audience of shapers show their appreciation of him.

Some minutes later, as the hands of shapers, great and small, tire, Maximus again approaches the podium. His hands are raised and he gestures to the crowd to cease their display of adulation and to allow him to continue with his speech. There is total silence now. The sense that even more important things than have been said already are yet to come is palpable amongst the shapers. Every eye is fixed hard upon their leader.

"Shapers of Slagway," he begins again, "much has been made of the fact that, in lesser towns and cities across the country, steps have been taken to put the Arts on the footing they deserve. Here," he says, raising a manual-like document, "I have '*The Dreary Report*', a blueprint for the development of the Arts in one of our larger cities."

Maximus is seen to stifle a yawn as he mentions the report in question. The mere mention of 'Dreary', coupled with the sight of Maximus' yawn, albeit stifled, plays havoc with the subconscious of many in the gathering and causes them to raise their hands to their mouths in an attempt to conceal the fact that they, unlike their noble leader, have been unable to control the urge to yawn. But, when they yawn, it is so artistically done that the very act itself redeems the situation. Dreary himself could hardly feel offended in the presence of such panache.

"Such steps as those to which I have alluded and, indeed, as those so expertly expounded upon by Dreary cannot, I feel, but fade into virtual insignificance in the light of what it is that I am about to announce for Slagway," he continues. Shapers of all shapes and sizes are seen to sit up shapily and sharpen the shapes in which they hitherto have found themselves unship-shapily sitting (yes – *sitting*!).

"*FARTS*", announces Maximus. There is a silence. Maximus has expected such. He knows it is far beyond the ability of the shapers seated there before him to even begin to decipher this important acronym.

"*FARTS*," he proclaims again, and this time, even louder.

The shapers look at one another, embarrassed by their ignorance of what a FART may be. They move their arsi magni, medii and pertly mini uncomfortably on their seats and whisper FART to all sides of them. There is confusion amongst the ranks. None has the knowledge to discern just what a FART may be and yet, none has the courage to inquire. None, that is, with the notable exception of Shaperus Dramatus, Master of the Vocative (Magister Vocativi).

"Maxime Magne," he begins (i.e. 'O Great Maximus'), "prithee tell us, humble shapers that we are, of the nature of this FART of which you speak."

And now the rumble of conversation mounts amongst the other shapers, as if somehow to suggest that, were it not for Dramatus' early intervention, each and every one of them would have requested just such an explanation.

Maximus clears his throat for yet another time, moves his spectacles from bridge to nosetip, then back to bridge again.

"The FART, my dear and fellow-Shapers, is, or *will*, I should really say, be a rare and wonderful creature emerging from the area of the Arts. I have, over the last number of years, spent many hours, oft times long into the summer nights, when the hot air could be stifling, discussing the institution of the FART with those in the higher echelons of power in this town's esteemed university, Universitas Slagwayi. There, much more than anywhere else that comes to mind, amongst our most venerable brothers in the world of academia, is the deepest understanding of the FART."

The shapers are enthralled at Maximus' eloquence. They hang onto his every word, milking it, embracing it, allowing it to massage and to make love to their minds, turning it over time and time again within their lesser intellects. None, as yet, has managed to discern quite what this FART, of which their great leader speaks, may be, but secretly they pray that, in the course of his address, Maximus may deem them sufficiently worthy to be told of its specific nature.

"The FART," Maximus continues, "is finally at hand. 'Fellow of the Arts', to give it its full and proper title. But FARTS, my fellow-Shapers, will be few and far between and that is something upon which our noble doctors of the Universitas are unanimously agreed. In our long and tireless discussions, we – the authorities of the Universitas and myself – have agreed that, once every five years, a new FART will be permitted; a new member will be received into the Circle of the FARTS. The FART, then, will be the pinnacle of existence in the world of the Arts and will, I am happy to inform the meeting, carry with it an honorary annual stipend of €18,999. This stipend will, of course, be index-linked."

There is rapturous applause in appreciation of all that Maximus has so *selflessly* done for the world of the Arts. Shapers of all sizes are seen to wipe tears (commensurate in size with their degree of shaperism) from their eyes. They are on their feet again and, for a second time, the chant of 'Maximus, Maximus, Maximus' resounds from wall to wall. Maximus, who has stepped back from the podium, suitably humbled by this demonstration of their appreciation and affection, comes forward once again. A clearing of the throat. A hush.

"Thank you, fellow-Shapers. I thank you." Again, a slight adjustment of the gold-rimmed, half-moon bifocals before proceeding. "Knowing me, as you so undoubtedly do, my fellow-Shapers, you will appreciate just how greatly honoured and surprised I was to have been told, just this very evening, by the President of the Universitas that I, the simple Maximus, am, on the occasion of the upcoming conferral, to be taken in as the first FART in the Circle."

Once again, Maximus speech is interrupted by the enthusiastic applause of all his fellow-shapers. Step back from the podium. Eventual waning of applause. Step forward yet again. Silence. Formulaic stuff!

"Believe me, my brothers," Maximus resumes, "that my happiness is not for myself, but for you, my fellow-Shapers. My membership as first FART taken into the Circle so satisfies me that it is as if you yourselves have been truly taken in."

They are on their feet again, applauding, chanting, revelling in the thought that they, in some small way, have contributed to the conferring of this honour on the highest form of shaper. Maximus sits back into his seat and all eyes follow him as he does so. Now Secundus has approached the podium again.

"Jaysus, dat's a grate bitta news, what! Mighty! Mighty altogedder! Well, fair play to ya, Maximus," says Secundus, and he gestures to the crowd, in that inimitable earthy way of his, encouraging them to continue their display of appreciation.

Some minutes pass and eventually the display of their

appreciation has come to an end. Our friend, the Fly, has mistimed his part in the ovation and likewise the delirium of his buzzing, as, in the suddenness of silence, finding himself caught in no-man's land between two walls, he draws the disapproving stare of shapers one and all. The Fly is fortunate that something as momentous as a final utterance from Maximus – who has now returned to the podium – draws the attention of the shapers away from him again.

"We have then, my fellow-Shapers, done well in the name of the Arts and each and every one of you has cause to feel pleased with your contribution and with the fact that this honour of the FART is every bit as much *your* honour as it is mine."

The Fly, now moved to a secluded corner where wall meets wall and both walls meet the ceiling, quietly titters, does a rapid head-count of the one hundred and thirty-seven shapers in attendance and tries to mentally divide €18,999 by that number. Drat! He can't do it. What a night, of all nights, to have left his feckin' calculator at home.

"Now, let us repair to *Knocked Down's* and celebrate what one can only term 'a milestone' in Slagway's championing of the Arts," concludes brave Maximus.

With that, the shapers are on their feet again and the thunderous chant of 'Maximus, Maximus, Maximus, Maximus' is of such an ilk that there remains not the slightest doubt as to the quality of the architectural stress factor of the walls, as much hailed, indeed, by one of their very own, i.e. Shaperus Constructus, at the time of building.

In the not-too-distant hostelry of Knocked Down's, the tumultuous chant of 'Maximus, Maximus' has reached all there. All ears within the walls of the well-famed tavern had earlier cocked themselves on hearing it and have, again now, lowered themselves, allowing the heads, to which they found themselves so luckily attached, engage their pints of black stuff once again. Only the ears of the gangly pink-necked journalist from THE OIRISH CHIMES – he, sent specially to attend the Meeting of the Shapers – have remained aloft.

"Ya can sittle down now, a mhaicín, dey'll be here in no time at all. Sure, didn't I tell ya dat dis'd be the bessht place ta git dem, hah?" says the diminutive figure beside the scribbler.

Our journalist smiles, satisfied with his perfect reading of the situation. He knows, of course, that the very best of anything that he has written has been garnered over a hefty shifting of the black stuff. There was no sense in bothering his arts in going down to the meeting when he could get them here. He checks the presence of the pencil stub above his ear and turns a new page of the notepad, which, all this time, he has, as it were, 'unthinkingly' left on view on the counter-top.

"Another pint there, Bartley," he beckons to the barman, "and you may also put another one up for Martineen here."

"Musha, fair play to ya," says Martineen. "Well, fair play to ya. Jaysus, dat's a grate payper dat ya'r workin' for – a grate payper."

4
An Elbow in the Arts

A hush comes over all in Knocked Down's when Secundus pushes open the door (in slips the Fly) and then, from outside, holds his arm across it until Maximus' frame comes forward and fills the opening. There is silence, then suddenly all inside burst into spontaneous applause. He enters and, as he does so, older men are seen to remove their soft caps – a Slagwayan courtesy at one time afforded as lowly a being as a parish priest and upwards, but nowadays specially reserved for a cardinal or pope. But this is Maximus – far greater in the town of Slagway than any mere red cap or pontiff.

The tumult respectfully and most biblically Red Seas itself before the Mighty Maximus, leaving a passage for him to make his way up to the bar. Some of the younger men hold their arms quite tightly around their girlfriends' waists, fearing that they might either be inclined to throw themselves before his feet or that his very presence might be sufficient to occasion a weakness in their white and virgin knees. Others of the younger men do likewise where their boyfriends are concerned.

Maximus reaches the bar and is quickly followed by Secundus and Administratus before the parted waters close themselves again to entrap many of the minnows of the entourage.

"Howaya, Maximus?" says Martineen.

"Mawwrtin," says Maximus, peering out across the top of his spectacles and looking down at the diminutive Martineen. "How awwr you? You'll have a pint. The usual, Bartley, and another pint for Mawwrtin at your convenience, if you please," he adds, in one long gush, underscoring his authority and his absolute expectation that anything that he decides will not be contested. Not, indeed, that our mac Martineen would even dream of putting anything other than his mouth in the way of the pulling of another pint.

"Ah shure, I will so, Maximus, and shure may ya never see the poor day."

"Good man, Mawwrtin, good man."

"Dis man here has come all da way from Bud...," the good Martineen begins to say, as he endeavours to introduce the pink and pencil-eared scribbler from the *CHIMES*. But Maximus has already moved away and headed for one of the partitioned booths at the far side of the hostelry. Now Secundus fills his place at the bar and, as in keeping with the pecking order of things, Administratus steps onto the spot previously heated by the clodhopper shoeleather on Secundus' feet.

"For da luvva God, will ya give it a ressht, Martineen! Don't ya know dat Maximus hash a lot on hish plate with dish new FART ting an' all," says the brothy Secundus, berating the little Slagwayman for his lack of sensitivity.

Yet again, the ears of our journalistic friend shoot up on hearing mention of the FART and, as they do, his almost-accidentally short-stubbed pencil makes its merry little way down off his lobular left lug and, unbeknownst to him, immerses itself in the deep black bowels of his newly ordered pint.

"FART?" says the man from the *CHIMES*, leaning forward now to introduce himself. "Umberto Duwell from *THE OIRISH CHIMES*," he says, and he extends his hand towards Secundus.

Secundus looks at him, then at his extended hand and keeps his own hands firmly entrenched in the deep dark pockets of his donkey jacket.

"Duwell? *OIRISH CHIMES*? Naw, doesshn't ring a bell at all at all."

"I'm here to cover your arts," Duwell tells him.

"Phwat? Cover my ar…"

"Yes, your arts AGM. The *CHIMES* is eager to do a feature on the plans for the coming year."

"The comin' year, ish it!" muses Secundus, as he looks more closely at the specimen before him. Something in the back of his mind is telling him that he has come across this man Duwell before. He sees his own face looking back at himself in the journalistically rounded glasses of the *CHIMES*man. Secundus, seldom allowed by Maximus to speak to scribblers of this kind, sees his chance to do so here. The chance of glory, the chance of fame, the chance, perhaps, of a profile on him in *THE OIRISH CHIMES*. But then the seeds of doubt raise their ugly little heads in Secundus' mind.

"War y'at da matin', war ya?" Secundus asks.

Duwell is perplexed. Not only has he not understood the question, but each and every syllable has succeeded in eluding his comprehension.

"I beg your pardon?"

"Da matin'. Ya war dare, I perfume?"

Duwell's confusion is even greater now. He has managed to garner the 'I' from Secundus' utterance, but all that's gone before and after it has not made the slightest sense whatsoever to him.

"I am terribly sorry, but would you mind so very much saying that somewhat more slowly for me?"

Administratus, who, with the probable exception of Maximus, is the only one in all of Slagway who can accurately interpret the speech of both protagonists here is about to intervene when his own vision of possible glory is cruelly whipped away from him by the frustrated Secundus:

"Ah, Jaysus, feck dis! Here, Martineen, a mhac, wuj ever in da name o' God tell us wat dis gobshite is sayin'?"

Martineen, summoned into service and, no doubt, seeing the prospect of yet another pint of the black stuff in the offing, springs from his stool and, with the seriousness demanded by the situation, presses his elfish little facesheen between those of the other two.

"Right den," says Martineen, directing what he has to say at Duwell, "wat is it yar askin' Secundus here?"

For reasons of the difference between the Slagwayan dialect as spoken by the quasi-Rabble in the town and that as spoken in the remote areas of the county – but only that – Duwell can more easily interpret Martineen's speech.

"Yes. Right," begins Duwell, somewhat hesitantly. "I'd like him to acquiesce to doing a piece with me on the Arts programme for the coming year."

"Ya wat?" says Martineen.

"I'd like him to acquiesce to …"

"Secundus, come here a minute," shouts Maximus from

the booth by the window. Secundus, oblivious to any other bidding but that of Maximus, abruptly leaves the company. His departure is timely, fortuitous, a function attributable to nothing if not divine intervention itself where Administratus is concerned.

The opportunity is seized. Administratus brushes Martineen aside, extends his hand towards Duwell and effects his own introduction.

"Administrratus. Shaperrus Administrratus, to be prrecise, or Y-J as I am increasingly being called these times," and, as he says so, he ruffles that semi-quiff of hair above his forehead that makes him that much more Yeatsean than any other he himself has ever seen.

"Ah, Y-J," says Duwell, as he shakes Administratus' hand.

"So, you've hearrd of me then," assumes Administratus.

"Well, no – at least I don't think so. Should I have heard of you?"

"Well, I rreally should have thought so. Perrhaps this will help you," and, as Administratus speaks, he turns in profile to allow Duwell see him in that light. Duwell is none the more enlightened than before, but the thought that there is the possibility of getting something quotable prompts him to keep this continued lack of recognition to himself.

"Ah, Y-J. Of course."

"Quite," says Y-J, and they immediately fall into conversation.

Elsewhere, Maximus and Secundus are in the throes of discussion, while Martineen, no longer the central figure of yore, but having, nonetheless, secured the two pints for his

service, is making his way towards Tomasheen – another of
the semi-Rabble whose claim to fame is that he, and he
alone, has, for twenty-two years, five months and three
days (come 11.09pm), kept the western end of the bar in
perfect balance.

This latter jewel of information is best explained,
perhaps; otherwise, that which is to ensue this night may
well, if the pun (which will later evidence itself) may be
excused, go totally over the reader's head: Tomasheen, or
as he was better known to the State, Tomasheen John
Mhicil Mhichael Antoine Sheáin Petro Stanislavsky (his
father being a Russian émigré who fled the Bolshies in
1917), had truly served his time at the bar in Knocked
Down's. Not only did the oaken stool, upon which he
would daily plant his not-inconsiderable Slagwayan arse,
bear a cheeky imprint in two halves, but the very counter
from which the brethren supped bore, at its western end,
the unmistakable indentation caused by Tomasheen's right
elbow.

Anyway and however, such was Tomasheen's
misfortune in recent times that his diligence and loyalty to
the cause of balancing the bar occasioned him to undergo
surgery on his aforementioned right elbow. It cut deep
when he was told by the surgeon, a prominent member of
the artistic community, known to most as Shaperus
Scalpelus, that the joint would have to be replaced by a
new, but guaranteed-to-last plastic elbow. (Those more
mathematically inclined may rest assured that the five
hours and thirteen minutes necessary for this operation
have been deducted from Tomasheen's overall service at
the bar and that the twenty-two years, five months and

three days alluded to above is an honest and accurate reflection of his term of service.)

In any event, Tomasheen has just recently begun to get the proper sense of feeling into the artificial joint and it is only in the last few weeks that he has felt at all confident again about his ability to unerringly balance the bar. Up to then, he has been feeling his way and pints have been seen to run off, at random, at either end of the bar in Knocked Down's. He smiles broadly now as he sees his old friend, Martineen, two pints aloft, begin to wend his way through the tumult and come in his direction.

At the centre of the bar the conversation has continued. Administratus has successfully impressed the insignificance of all but one of the upcoming Arts activities upon Duwell from the *CHIMES*.

"Yes, a Rreadink, this night ffortnight, by one of ourr morre illustrrious memberrs of the countrry's wrriting frraterrnity."

"This night fortnight, you say?"

"Yess. Therre is alrready grreat clamourr forr tickets forr the event."

"Mmm!" says Duwell.

"And it would, indeed, do yourr carreerr in jourrnallissm no harrm whatsoeverr werre you to be therre to coverr it on the night."

Duwell's real interest in the event is somewhere between none and less than none, but the hope that his contact with Administratus may somehow yet facilitate a meeting with Maximus prompts him to carry through the charade on which he has embarked. He reaches into the inside pocket of his tweedy-twee jacket and takes out his dearie-diary. Once out, the removal of his elbow from the bar to open the diary causes a slight imbalance in the way of things. This prompts Tomasheen at the western end to compensate somewhat by not leaning so heavily with his new equipment. As Fate would cruelly have it, however, at almost one and the same time, Martineen has reached his old friend's end of the counter and he plonks down both pints just west of Tomasheen's much-talked of elbow. The man of Russian extract is caught unawares, feels a second tremor and, in his effort to effect a further compensation in so short a time, he over-balances the bar and causes almost everything just east of centre to come lobbing in his direction.

Suddenly, Knocked Down's is in unprecedented disarray. Pints of black stuff are hurtling through the air, some with the decency to remain within their glasses as they travel, others spilling forth in wild abandon. Frantic efforts by many at the counter to seize caps, spectacles and other sundry items in mid-flight add to the commotion, causing some to fall face down onto the floor and others to violently bang heads against one another. Those few who are of the quick-thinking brigade of shapers lend their weight to the eastern end of the bar in the hope that their efforts, somehow, may restore whatever order may have previously existed, but this, if anything, simply compounds the situation. Eyes bulge, mouths are agape and limbs scamper in directions never before thought possible.

The unfortunate Duwell might well manage what the mêlée has to throw at him were it not for matters underfoot. Yes, indeed, though all too late, he does see the set of false teeth, which has parted company with some gummy gob to which they properly belong, coming in his direction. Before he even has the time to think of how he may avoid them, they plant themselves deep into his fleshy neck, occasioning great quantities of blood to spurt forth. But underfoot – that which he has absolutely not a snowball's chance in hell of avoiding – a glass eye, formerly the occupant of the left eye socket of poor ould Tomasheen's deceased émigré father and long since kept by his plastic-elbowed son as the sole memento of his old man, has, as Tomasheen has hit the deck, spilled out of the pocket of his waistcoat and deviously tra-la-la-la-laad itself in Duwell's direction.

Duwell's delayed reaction to the teeth embedding themselves in his neck now causes him to jump in shock, timely allowing the said ocular sphere to maliciously roll in under his left peg. As the scribbler comes back to earth, his sole makes contact with the rolling glass orb and he is violently catapulted into reverse somersault mode, causing first his feet and then his head to viciously make contact with the solid brass oil lamp which hangs from the rafter overhead. The double wallop has rendered him unconscious, prostrate on the floor and totally oblivious to the fact that, even worse again, the killer blow has yet to come.

Other than Martineen, who's busily trying to entrap anything of liquid-kind that he can, the carnage is substantial: Tomasheen's elbow is gone for good this time, Maximus and Secundus are not the better of the shock and Administratus, dishevelled, is rummaging on the floor in search of his spectacles. Alas, most foully dealt of all is poor Duwell. Well, Duwell did well, but not quite well enough. That pencil, that snide and short-stubbed pencil that had callously concealed itself and stayed within the darkened depths of the pint of black stuff until its moment of retribution was at hand: there it stood, its point embedded smack dab in the middle of poor, dead, ne'er Duwell's forehead. Never before in Knocked Down's was there such a case of Porter most Foul.

Still, all is not lost. Those of importance – Maximus, Secundus and our dear Administratus – have come through relatively unscathed. So too Martineen, whose loss would not be mourned, but it is, perhaps, of use to us at a later date that he should survive the holocaust for now. And, so too, of course, the Fly. But oh, ochón again, poor Tomasheen – he of the perfect balance, whose Russian father before him had seen such hardship – Tomasheen has not survived the cut. Suffice it to say that, in times to come, in places in the town where this night of sad destruction may be spoken of, it is not unthinkable that he should be fondly known as he who, when push came to shove, quite simply did not know his Arts from his Elbow.

5
The (K)Night of the Rreadlink

"Arts! What is the Arts?" the writer asks. "A reworked form of 'Star'," he assures his audience and then proceeds to tell how it was stolen from O'Casey ('What is the stars, what is the stars?') and cleverly – very cleverly – rearranged by none other than himself, this genius of a visitor to the literary circles of Slagway.

A loud knock of brass on brass on the ground-floor Georgian door disturbs the listeners, impinges on the minds of those who have come to hear this phenomenon read from his latest work. He is a phenomenal reader, they think, inside their little heads, feeling, in their decision, that they have grown and spread and flown wings of their own, far beyond the somewhere-else-decided-fact that yes, he is a phenomenal writer. They have made their *own* decision: yes, he is a phenomenal *reader*.

Brass on brass again downstairs! The writer has not heard it. The writer who is reader has not heard. But his listeners cringe: it is a member of the Rabble knocking on the door below, insensitive to the fact that Art is taking place in this hallowed room, in this bastion of bliss, high above the level of those who do not know, of those incapable of knowing.

Administratus, perched importantly beside the reading writer-reader, cocks his ears. He is like a rabbit who has felt the vibration of the approaching dog's heartbeat as it

35

thumps against the earth. He tutt-tutts – artistically, of course – and pushes back the rounded glasses on his nose. The listeners watch him, thinking how much, facially, he looks like a cross between Yeats and Joyce, and knowing for sure now that the right man – (no, no, in their minds they now pc-ally correct themselves) – the right *person* got the job. He rises now and moves swathingly towards the door, feigning discretion in his movement, while, at the same time, knowing that he has done enough to draw the eyes of those gathered in the name of the Arts towards him. But for an accident of birth – two left feet – he could have been a dancer. A great da*w*ncer.

As he nears the bottom of the stairs, the lesser of his two left feet makes contact with the other and he is jettisoned forward onto the hallway floor. Prostrate on the ground, he looks around him. "Fuck," he says out loud, then quickly raises himself and checks that there is no one on the stairs behind him. Phew! No one has heard him. They are all artistically enthralled by their writer-reader who is guesting especially for them. They are all aware that their Lancelot has left them to save the situation. He checks himself. What he really meant was 'Fock'. He would make a point of rehearsing that one.

Brass on brass yet again. It is as if it is inside his head now, he is so near the door. He composes himself, smoothes back his hair and fluffs up the silken crimson handkerchief in the breast pocket of his elegant, off-grey evening jacket. It is Italian. He had deliberately paid a fortune for it. And that was only for the handkerchief! Artistically, he opens the door and speaks at the same time. His timing is impeccable. If he could do this with his feet, his two left feet, he might have been that da*w*ncer.

"Ssshhh! Therre is a rreadink goink on," he says, beratingly, revelling in the deep resonant sound of his own voice. He liked it even better when he rehearsed it in the bathroom. There, unknown to anybody else, he could press his hand against his ear and really hear the sound of his own voice inside his head. Rrressonnannce!

"Therre is a rreadink goink on," he remonstrates once again.

"How 'ya! Is did Number Farty?"

"Noo, itt is nott! Thhis is Nomber Thhirrty Thhhrrreee," he responds, his sense of authority being commensurately augmented by his ability to rroll his Rs and to terrify his Ts with aspiration. "Nnow, if you don't mind, thherre iss a rreadink goink on."

The door is shut. The threat of Rabble is once again abated. Our hero mounts the stairs, pausing, in a practiced fashion, by one of the darker glass-fronted paintings that adorn the staircase. This is the one that, as he has learned, allows him see his own reflection, check his hair and confirm the fluffy-uppedness of his Italian, crimson handkerchieffi. He rounds the banister onto the first floor landing and is about to scale the thirteen steps that will redeliver him into the arms of culture, when, unexpectedly, it happens once again.

Brass on brass, and even louder than before. He stops. His eyes bulge. He has decided they should bulge: it shows emotion and a range of artistic temperament that is expected of him by the others, or, if not by them, then by himself. The irises almost make contact with the lenses in his spectacles. He turns now and bounds back down the steps, this time carefully pointing the toes of his two left feet in opposite directions as he moves. The trundling is heard above, much more so than any of the knocker's efforts. He cannot know it, but he himself has succeeded in bringing the reader, the guest writer-reader, *his* guest writer-reader, to a halt.

He opens the door once again, sure that, this time, he can surpass his earlier ability to rroll his Rs and terrify his Ts. He lunges forward, but there is no one there. No one to whom he can announce that 'Thhhherrrre isss a rrreadinkkk goinkkk on'. He stands out on the pavement, looks up and down the semi-lighted street and satisfies himself by mentally rehearsing that 'fock' of earlier resolution. Thank God his little faux pas on that one had not been overheard. It must be practised. It *must* be practised. As he closes the door again and makes his way back up the stairs, his mind is filled with the possibilities of what he might do with that word. 'Ffockk', 'effokk', 'ffockke', 'effuck' … no, no! That 'U' would have to go. It is too much like the Rabble babble!

Later, when all have survived the uncouth Storming of the Bastion, they gather in the lower drawring room for drinkies, sharing their impressions of the reading, forwarding their ideas, or idears, hearing others but listening only to their own. Our hero stands beneath the splendid crystal chandelier. He is so tall that the lowest crystal globule fiddles with his hair, dancing here and there on his dawncer's head. His guest, the writer-reader, is quite quiet. It is interesting for him to hear the many elements contained in his writing that he had not intended, elements that he, himself, could not see.

"Yes, yes, rrathher significant, I thhought, thhat you should synthhesise the mystical and the existentialist in thhat fashion," our hero says, by way of *simple* comment on the reading.

The writer-reader tries to keep up with this. After all, it is he who has written the piece. But, even he now can see the Yeats-Joyce resemblance (the Y-J factor, as the aficionados have come to know it) in Administratus' face – that which all others in the room have long since identified. But the writer-reader is a simple or, at least, *uncomplicated* man. His pronunciation could do no better than to utter 'fuck' as 'fuck'. He is amazed at himself, enthralled at all that he has written that he had not known he'd written. Perhaps, sometimes, the writer-reader begins to think, I *am* outside myself; perhaps Y-J is right about this blend of the mystical and the existentialist which he has identified!

"You see," our hero says, "it rreminds me somewhat of the famous RRussian authhorrs – most parrticularrly the more incisive ones, the more cutting, more surgically inclined in use of language – like, say, Ivanknackinknockingemoff ..."

He is interrupted, appropriately *cut off*. One of the ladies – she who, amongst her coffee morning set, claims to be the one to have first noticed the Y-J factor in our hero's face – approaches, dares to touch Administratus on the elbow.

"I think you handled that earlier little interruption quite ma*w*rvellously, Y-J."

His head swells – noticeably – so much so that the crystal globule that has dared to flirt with his slinky hair is now forced to lie flat on top of it. Lucky crystal globule! This, our Y-J knows, is what handling such matters is all

about. This is what makes his effective administering of
whatever it is that he administers so very worthwhile ...
fulfilling ... important. What a pity Shaperus Maximus
could not make it there tonight. Indeed, it would have
done our hero no harm – no harm at all – for him to have
seen him handle the situation. He blushes now at the
thought: what if Shaperus Maximus had followed him out
just in time to see his da*w*ncer's feet perform the
unintended!? Phew! It is, perhaps, better that he was not
there after all. Some one of the others – maybe our friend
who prides herself on having first identified the Y-J factor
– could discreetly let Shaperus Maximus know of our
hero's feet – I mean 'feat'. Yes, that could be arranged. After
all, our hero does have his *vays UND meanz*.

The glory of his deed being recognised carries him
through the remainder of the evening. Such soirées are not
about writers, or readers, or even writer-readers. They are
about effectively handling one, or all, or simply some of
same. Our hero feels effective, handlingly effective. The
writer-reader has been effectively dispatched in the
company of the Y-J factor originator. She will ensure that he
locates the hotel, or better still, the hotel bed which has
been effectively reserved for the occasion. She will ensure
that he is satisfied, for she is one who knows that there are
only two things better than a writer who is satisfied: one,
dear reader, is a writer-reader who is satisfied; the other is
that the satisfier of a writer-reader is quite satisfied that she
has satisfied a writer-reader!!!

Y-J rests against the heavy Georgian door then. Yes, he
has done well. He has done damned Yeatsingly and
Joycingly well. He moves down the hallway and up the

steps of the stairs, then stops. He knows, though he has not counted, that he is on the seventh step. There, beside him, on the wall, as proof of his undoubted intuition, is the dark, glass-fronted painting. A glance. My goodness! I do look like Yeats and Joyce together, he thinks. He lingers a while, then moves on up the steps, reminding himself that sometime, before too long, he must look at that painting – just to know, for the betterment of Art, who the artist is and what it is that is in it.

On the landing, just before the final thirteen steps, he stops. His underwear has somehow gathered itself between the cheeks of his posterior, causing him discomfort. Worse again, that pimple on his arsus magnus is bothering him again. The need to scratch is almost unbearable; the urge is not resisted. There, he has scratched, but now it needs more scratching. He scratches more and more until the itch has been defeated. It dawns on him that someone had told him – no, no, not *just someone*. It must have been a writer, an important writer, he is sure. Yes, that was it, of course. Some important writer had written that when a pimple's itch had been abated, it was a sign that blood had at last been drawn. He works his fingers beneath the bunched-up article of underwear, releases it and spreads it evenly again across the cheeks of his bisected pulchritude.

Oh, my God! The blood, the underwear! Oh, that's right, no cause for worry now. He has just remembered his Italian, silken crimson handkerchieffi and he knows he never wears that deftly chosen piece without his matching brieffis. No problem. No stain. Crimson on pure crimson.

Brass on brass downstairs. He is rattled for a second,

but quickly composes himself. "Ffocckk off," he says, and he listens to the echo bounce to and fro from wall to ceiling and back to wall again, affirming for him that he has finally got it right. Plenty of 'f', plenty of 'k', and feck all 'u' at all.

Farewell Duwell: Poetica's Fifteen Seconds of Feculent Fecundity

Winter bit hard in the western town of Slagway and, for the first time in the living memory of even the oldest denizens of this revered and ancient haven of the Arts, many of the more seasoned shaperi were not to be seen at the various off-season soirées that usually would carry them artistically through Springtime once again. For those less established in the ways of shaperism, it was an unexpected opportunity for them to bring themselves to the notice of such luminaries as Secundus and Administratus and, indeed, should the first and fairest FART of all deign to grace an occasion with his prescriptive presence, of none other than bold Maximus himself.

It was, perhaps, the untimely misfortune that befell the ill-fared-well Duwell – he of THE OIRISH CHIMES – that occasioned the season's last sizeable coming together of the major shapers. Though far from any standing or renown, despite it being mooted in some hostelries that Duwell was soon to have been offered some piss-Artless weekly column with possible minority appeal, and quite poorly written in a language known only to a few (Secundus being of their number), the Slagway literati sensed it *politically wise* to acknowledge his departure in some shaper-form. Though long since interred in his native Budlin, a remembrance ceremony was deemed appropriate. Poetica had been summoned to give of her best. Indeed, it was also thought that she might even have a poem.

Subsequently, reports in all the Slagway papers informed the non-attendants at the ceremony (i.e. Rabble and less important shaperi) that yes, indeed, Poetica had done the business with her specially composed tribute to the pencil stub-stabbed stalwart of the Arts. Most of them, indeed, saw fit to offer copy of her creation on their front pages: 'Elegy written in a Slagway Churchyard'. On the day, her delivery was nothing if not exquisite, commanding silence from one and all who were in attendance. It was only during the mesmeric epitaph that any interruption was to be heard, and that itself was perfectly understandable: it was a mixture of sigh and cry from our own brave Martineen who, at the final fence, had to give way to the welling sentiment evoked in him by the memory of his stubby-pencilled pint-purchasing penmate from the *CHIMES*. And so:

Elegy written in a Slagway Churchyard

The Slagway curfew tolls the knell of parting day,
The lowing herd winds slowly oe'r the lea,
The shapers homeward plod their weary way,
And leave the world to darkness and to me.

Now fades the glimmering landscape on the sight
And Slagway air a solemn stillness holds,
Save where I, Poetica, write in dimming light
And ivory tinklings lull the distant folds.

[And then Blah-de Blah Blah Blah – poetically, of course –
for several tens of verses until ...]

The Epitaph

Here rests his head upon the lap of Earth,
A youth, to Fortune and to Fame unknown;
Fair Science frowned not on his humble birth
And Melancholy marked him for her own.

Large was his bounty and his soul sincere;
            [it was here that Martineen's eyes showed first signs of glistening]
Heaven did a recompense as largely send:
He gave to Misery all he had – a tear
                [and now a tear, predominantly black in colour, with a soft and
                        creamy white froth, rolled out onto Martineen's cheek]
He gain'd from Heaven, 'twas all he wished – a friend.
                        [it was at this point that sigh and cry seemed to come
                            together to form Martineen's heartfelt sob]

"Pottery of da highessht arrder! Pure underadulterated genius!" said Secundus. He was near enough to Poetica on the day to ensure that his utterance reached her ears. She smiled at him. Secundus was mindful of the fact that, at the shapers' AGM, he had overtly given her praise with a similar comment and that the Brownie points merited on that occasion would be handsomely added to by this extra little sycophantic effort. It disturbed his equilibrium even to ponder the steaminess of the payment she might feel it appropriate to make and the prospect that, after such payment had been made, he might lie upon her – a man spent and drained, his head nestled between her fulsome, heaving breasts, and his eyes simultaneously looking in different directions, so as to savour fully the beauty of the moment.

Indeed, Secundus' prospects of a Slagway Lay of his

very own were dealt no harm whatsoever when his words were quoted verbatim in *The Slagway Atomiser*, just beneath its publication of the poem. Comment like that being so publicised would surely please Poetica no end and that, in turn, should make her all the more grateful to Secundus and that, in turn, again could mean … oh, my God, my God, my God … sure, I'm not a well man even at the thought of it …

Poetica, for her part, though delighted with the perceived brilliance of her composition for ne'er-do-well Duwell's farewell, and even more so with the exposure in *The Atomiser*, *The Turbine*, *The Sentiment* and other local rags, was at pains to convey the fear that the time dedicated to the honing of the 'Elegy' would seriously set back her schedule on the completion of her eagerly awaited ten-poem collection. It was conceivable, she had been heard to comment, that the writing of the remaining nine poems could take up to another ten years. However, never to despair, she quickly added that she already had seven titles for the projected poems (a good year's work in itself) and, indeed, was very quickly receptive to the suggestion (again by Secundus — even more Brownie points, bejay) that the 'Elegy', being so excellently Gray, could surely be included as one, if not two or three, of the poems.

And so it was that the intrepid reporter finally went down, felled by his own self's faithful pencil stub, the acridity of which had, in ne'er Duwell's own *CHIMING* times, felled many a mortal far greater than himself. Never more the right to reply, but then, where Duwell was concerned, such a right had never been afforded. Ask no corner, seek no favour. And so, farewell, Duwell. How well the world will wail while willing wailers wail well over you. What? No feckin' wailers! Well!

It was, then, these two events – Umberto Duwell's last farewell and Poetica's rarefied commemoration of his having been ... whatever it actually was that he had been – that marked the winter any different to the many that had gone before. All else was of the banal. Yet again, this winter, another aspirant to the status of shaper minor had been found dead one frosty Monday morning. He had, apparently, while coming from a heavy session of sessioning, slipped on a banana skin in Slagway's Latin Quarter. An autopsy, conducted by none other than the hitherto unmentioned Shaperus Coroneratus, showed that asphyxiation had been the cause of death: two glass milk bottles – the only contents of the guitar case which he had been always seen to carry – had, apparently, jettisoned themselves into the air when the guitar case opened in the fall and plummeted down again, one striking him on the forehead, the other ramming itself neck-first into his mouth and lodging in his gullet.

Unlike Duwell, no pomp and ceremony for our banana-skidding friend; simply the consolation to the Slagwayan community that, at last, they knew what it was that he had carried in his guitar case this last twenty-three years or so. Two sparkling glass milk bottles – the milk a little sour, of course. Still, nothing better to make a bit of a musical rattle when that is what is needed. Ah well, 'tis an ill wind ...

7
A Dangerous Liaison

Ill winds will wilfully wend wily ways within well-walled havens such as Slagway and times of quiet, much more than any other, are fodder to their blowing. So it was that, despite the apparent inactivity of wintertime, things unknown to shapers were very much afoot. The Rabble, scourge of Artdom and of all that any decent shaper ever stood for, had, after years of enduring oppression, struck what many would have thought a most unlikely, yet dangerous liaison. Those to the far west of Slagway, who lived in the permanently sun-filled region known as Moracenna, had also long been spurned and deigned inferior by those who owned the arts.

But now the Rabble and the Moracennans had joined forces and had resolved to make a concerted effort through the winter months to devise a plan that would finally put an end to the acts of degradation and exclusion to which they had, for many years, been subjected by the Slagwayans.

An invaluable asset to both sides in this joint effort was a knowledge amongst the Rabble of Garlic, the Moracennan tongue, while many of the Moracennans also had a more-than-passable competence in Rabble-babble. Regular clandestine meetings and discussions had, in the course of the months, resulted in the inadvertent emergence of a hybrid of both languages, now known as

Garble, and it was agreed between the partners that, for reasons of security and secrecy, all future plans should be discussed in the new tongue only.

As happens in these matters, the question of leadership arose and it was here that a most unlikely character (though one whose possible emergence had earlier been presaged) came to prominence. None other than the bould and brave Martineen, sponger-in-chief of pints and one-time friend of Tomasheen, great balancer of the bar, showed unexpected qualities.

"Brudders," he told a meeting of the partners one night in the cold depths of January, "I've seen it all, like, ya know what I mean. Jaysus, sure I've sshtood at the bar wit the besssht of dem, like, ya know – Administratus and Secundus. Sure, even Maximus hisself has had great time for me like, ya know. And the other poor ould shitehawk from the *CHIMES* – Duwell, wasshn't it? Musha, God help him! Sure, he was what you might call the 'ultimate gobshite'."

Martineen could tell that they were well impressed by the term 'ultimate gobshite'. Sure, God knows, when he thought on it himself, it did have something of a sophisticated ring to it. Yeah, a real sophisticated ring – what one might truly call a *CHIME*.

Martineen's personal knowledge of the various characters from top to bottom of the continuum of shaperism was most certainly deemed invaluable to the new alliance, but even more importantly, he had been privy, by virtue of his fringe status (*status fringi*), to much of their planning for the upcoming season, as loosely – and oft times very loosely – discussed in Knocked Down's. Even now, given the secrecy

of the new organisation, there was no reason why
Martineen might not still mingle amongst the shapers from
time to time. He had already told the newly founded
Rabble-Moracennan Society (which title, incidentally, it
was agreed, should alternate with the Moracennan-Rabble
Society on a cyclical six-monthly basis, thereby showing
real equality in the dismemberment of the arts) of the
institution and nature of the FART, of Administratus'
wider plans for the year ahead and, most particularly, of
the theme of this year's big parade.

'Fresh Air,' the gathering mused the night that
Martineen told them, their reaction not unlike that of the
shapers themselves when first they too had heard it
announced. Then there were wild guffaws of laughter
amongst the Rabble-Moracennans, but this was quickly
replaced by an air of seriousness, culminating in a second
– though, this time, far more serious – uttering of 'Fresh
Air'.

"Da very ting, me brudders," said Martineen, "and nun
udder."

Unbeknownst to any of the Rabble or the Moracennans,
or even the Rabble-Moracennans, a constant in their midst
at any and all of their meetings – from day one, indeed –
was none other than our friend of great ubiquity, the Fly.
He, of all who lived within the environs of Slagway, though
none could ever have had reason to suspect so, was, at
one and the same time, the most travelled and most
knowledgeable. On the very night that Martineen had
decided to impart his knowledge of things FARTian and
things Fresh Airian, our mate, the Fly, was so excited at
what might be in the offing that he so feverishly rubbed his

forelegs together with delight that the smell of burning occasioned by the friction of his spindly limbs wafted its way to many a Moracennan and equally as many a Rabbleian nostril.

"Jaysus, is dar sometin' burrnin' in dish plache or is it jussht dat me noshthrils is playin' thricks on me, whah?" asked John James Joseph Michael Bartley Petereen, the acknowledged (though unofficial) leader of the Moracennan faction within the secret coalition.

"Dar's sometin' afoot all right," says Stepheneen. The said Stepheneen, Martineen's newly appointed right-hand man from within the Rabble contingent, was another one-time friend of the ill-fated Tomasheen of the not-too-distant past. Then all present began to sniff with a not-inconsiderable degree of deliberateness and gradually raised their eyes and nostrils in the direction of the ceiling.

The Fly, being the shrewd wee bugger he was, skilfully perched himself on the upper part of the light bulb and emitted a very gentle 'phew' as the brothers beneath him lowered both their gazes and their smelling apparati once again and carried on with their meeting.

The Fresh Air theme was discussed further, all in attendance gleaning what they could from Martineen's presentation, then questioning even further until such time as their capacity to absorb any more information was at bursting point. A decision was made to repair to *The Locks*, a hostelry not dissimilar to Knocked Down's, but one which was very much on the opposite side of the street and would decidedly have nothing to do with anything that was not one hundred and twenty-five and a half per cent unpretentious. Indeed, the decision to make The Locks

their watering hole had been unanimous and when, on the
occasion of the taking of that decision, one of the Rabble-
Moracennan number was heard to ask, "Now, like, would
dat one hundred and twenty-five and a half per cent
unpretentiousness mean more than totally unpretentious?",
he was quickly reassured by Martineen that, "Yes, very
definitely more than totally unpretentious, if not, indeed,
even more than that again." Suffice it to say that the
questioner was, at the very least, absolutely and totally
mathematically satisfied – that level of satisfaction reading,
presumably, no more and certainly no less than one
hundred and twenty-five and a half percentage points on
the Rabble-Moracennan Scale of Satisfaction.

Of course, the Fly – never one to miss an opportunity –
also took himself to the said alehouse and mingled in
the various little groups of the membership that dotted
themselves at the many tables in the establishment. He was
fortunate in that, on his mother's side, his great grandfather
had been an African tsetse fly of the genus *Glossina* and his
grandmother an anopheles mosquito of the dreaded genus
Plasmodium. This ensured, several generations back, that
any progeny resulting from their and their offspring's
procreative efforts were guaranteed, if nothing else, to be
veritable polyglots. This being the case, the fusion of
ancient Moracennan Garlic and urban Rabble-Babble to
form the new tongue Garble presented little difficulty
whatsoever to the Fly. It was a certainty – indeed, what
Martineen in his wisdom would term 'a more than one
hundred per cent certainty' – that nothing of linguistically
important content would get by the intrepid winged
sleuth.

From all the Fly could garner from his eavesdropping (Jaysus, what's that in me pint?!) – no, no *eavesdropping*, as in 'listening in' – the major matter of interest at the different tables seemed to be the devising of a plan to scupper the Fresh Air parade of the upcoming August, some seven months hence. Of course, there would be other acts of sabotage between now and then, but, in many respects, these could be viewed, at best, as being secondary and it was generally agreed that they would constitute invaluable practice in the ways of discommoding.

8
Secundus finally gets his

How timely! How beautifully, ironically and seductively timely that our trojan, Secundus, should be about the business of finally getting around to having himself satisfied at the selfsame time that those of whom he did not yet even know should be conspiring to bring about his and many others' downfall.

The bould Secundus, workhorse extraordinaire that he is renowned to be, has stayed back in the workshop long after his fellow-artistic brothers have gone to their homes, or to some others' homes, perhaps. For the last five hours, he has had the place totally to himself and, high up on the indoor scaffold, he has busied himself with fixing his sizeable nuts to the ends of the numerous metal poles which, come August of the year, will serve as lengthy retaining bars for the myriad displays along the Fresh Air theme. Even at this stage, he can envisage the onlookers' reaction to what they will see on the day:

"Jaysus, look at Secundus' nuts on the ends of the poles," he can imagine the men along the streets say. And then the women – wives, widows, sweethearts and would-be vestal virgins – will gasp and swoon and then be heard to comment, *"God, nuts never neared nuttin' like dem nuts before."*

It is as Secundus tightens the final of his nuts onto the end of yet another length of pole that Poetica speaks. He has been totally unaware of her having come into the workshop.

"What marvellous nuts you have there, Secundus!"

The very sound of her voice excites him. He turns, knowing that, at last, the moment of long-promised satisfaction might well be at hand.

"Poetica, bejay! What's dat ya war sayin'?"

She is clad in a deep-cut gown of crimson silk and a light, black lace mantilla rests gently on her head of darkened curls. From his perch, he can see a damn sight more of his Poetica than many a man has ever seen before. She looks up at the gallant Secundus, his legs spread-eagled high above her. "Your nuts, Secundus, they are as sweet as the kernel of a hazel that has fallen from the bough."

Bejaysus, thinks Secundus to himself, that has to be some class of a poetic compliment, or if not, then he doesn't know his nuts from apples. He immediately wraps his hands around the nearest upright, slithers down the scaffolding and, as he lands on the workshop floor, Poetica moves quickly towards him. His nose attends to the strong smell of drink from her breath, while his eyes fasten hard onto the cleavage of her scantily covered bosom.

"Poetica, I –"

His speech is abruptly (though most poetically, it must be said) interrupted as the sensuous carver of occasional verse pulls the mighty workhorse towards her and firmly plants her lips hard on his. So unexpectedly enrapt is our man that any residual thought of further tightening of his nuts does not even enter his head or – even more fortuitously still where he's concerned – any other part of his anatomy. As Poetica parts her lips now and her tongue engages his, she presses her body against him. Secundus' peepers widen in delight and he sees her green eyes spiral in a fashion that he has never seen before. Then, she steps back a second, wriggles her slender body, and her gown of crimson silk slowly, teasingly, slips down off her voluptuous breasts onto her hips and then, from there, right down to the ground, sensuously caressing every inch of her soft whiteness as it goes. But for the lace mantilla, which still sits unruffled on her head, she is as naked as the day she came out of the womb – that glorious day of days, when the doctor, checking the baby's vital apparatus, declared to her mother that "It's a ... it's a ... it's a POET".

Again she comes forward, slips her creative poet's hands inside the besotted Secundus' overalls and draws him to the ground. There is much rummaging of clothing, a wrestling and a rolling, though, despite all the frenetic movement, Poetica still manages to perfectly balance her little black mantilla on her head. Then, finally, they are as each would have the other be, and now Secundus finds his breath is racing and increasingly he feels the need to cry out:

"Ah ... ahh ... ahhh ... ahhhh ..."

"Ahhhhh-chooooo!" the brave Martineen cries out over in The Locks, as, at last, the sneeze that has been mounting in him vents itself and, at one and the same time, contaminates the pints and half ones of those sitting with him at the table. Our friend, the Fly, though several tables away, hops in shock from his perch of comfort atop of the rim of a Moracennan's glass and makes upwards towards the safety of the ceiling. As he climbs, he hears what, for all the world, could be thought to be the repetitive beginnings of another sneeze somewhere far distant from The Locks. Now he attends somewhat more deliberately to what it is he hears: "Ahhh ... ahhhh ... ahhhhh ..." My God, it sounds like the voice of Secundus. He is in distress, the good Fly thinks. And, just as he realises this, one of the company decides to call it a night. "It's a night," says the parting member, rising from his seat, throwing back the remnants of his pint and heading for the door. The Fly, a long-time master of deft timing, watches for his chance and, as the said party opens the door to exit, out goes the little bugger via the aerial route.

"Hasta la vista, baby," says the Fly under his breath, et nil cognitus est de fuga sua.

In no time at all even the prattle rattle of hybrid Garble back at The Locks is distant to the ears of the Fly. His mind now is focused on his mission and that, he has skilfully discerned, is very much centred on Secundus' city centre workshop. As he nears the building, the groaning sound has waned, but he notices what he thinks is either smoke or steam emerging from the rooftop of the building. His initial impulse is to veer off and head for Shaperus Arsonus' place so that he, in his capacity as City Fire Chief, can activate the services. But then the Fly thinks twice of doing so and decides that he will check a little more closely before occasioning alarm bells to be rung.

On the rooftop now, the most obvious port of entry seems to be the chimney. He swoops down the chimney pot and then beyond, encountering on his way a veritable mist of what is unquestionably a mixture of steam and smoke. When he reaches the bottom, he is gasping for breath and is more than a little relieved to find that there is no fire in the grate. He rests now on the hearthstone, slowly drawing his breath – in slowly – out slowly, in slowly – out slowly, in slowly – out sl… Wait a minute! What's this he sees across the workshop floor from him? He scurries to the seclusion of the brass companion set that stands at one end of the hearth and then peers out between the poker and the tongs. Well, holy and divine! In feckin'-slowly, out-slowly is right! If it isn't the one and only Secundus lying there bollock-naked, flat on top of Slagway's prima Poetica.

Secundus' head is exactly as he himself had liked to envisage it, safely ensconced in the considerably deep valley between Poetica's bountiful breasts, steam steadily rising from him and his arse unashamedly propped up to the world of possibility. As for Poetica, she lies beneath him, her head to one side of the secondary shaper's as she deliberately draws long and hard and slowly on a Gauloise cigarette and then expels the inhaled smoke from her lungs again. Between drags on the weed, she seems to be in the act of composing, lowly chanting words which, despite his best efforts, the poor Fly simply cannot interpret.

"Well, feck it," says the Fly, and he decides to draw up a little closer to the scene of action-past and action-present. He lands down on top of Poetica's pertly placed mantilla which, throughout all the twisting and turning and wrestling and heaving of whatever it has been that she and Secundus have been about, has remained primly and perfectly in place. The Fly gently makes his way out to the front edge of the mantilla and, from his new vantage point now, he sees the bisected rolling hills of mammaries and buttocks down below him. Being as he is, a healthy and upstanding heterosexual winged male, the temptation to linger longer on Poetica's generous endowment is that much greater, but then something in his breeding gains precedence over that. It is impossible for him to ignore what, for successive generations, has been in his genes: the warrior fly in him bursts to the fore. He knows that, back in their respective homes, Secundus and Poetica have loyal partners who know nothing of the deceit that has happened here this night and he feels obliged – great descendant of the tsetse and the anopheles mosquito that he is – to avenge the honour of absent spouses.

He eyes the dead centre of Secundus' right buttock, ensuring that his focus is as precise as it can be. Then he steps back momentarily from the edge of the mantilla, places most of his weight on his two hind legs and both physically and mentally winds himself up like a hornet. And finally the swoop. His effecting of the raid is as expert as the best of any Special Forces SAS or SWAT team may have carried out. The sting is sharp and deep, firmly embedded now into the buttock and guaranteed to occasion malicious festering in the passage of time.

"Chrissht, I'm sstunged!" yells Secundus, abruptly hopping up off Poetica and causing her to completely lose the line of poetry with which she has been toying for many minutes past. "Some little bashhtard of a ting is after stingin' me in da feckin' arse."

Of course, by now, the Fly has hightailed it by the short route back across the workshop floor and is safely ensconced yet again behind the companion set on the hearth.

"Jaysus, have a look at dat, Poetica, will ya?" says Secundus, turning his posterior towards her so that she may inspect the point of penetration. "Can ya see anythin' dare, can ya, can ya?"

If ever their little roll in the workshop was going to lead to unexpected intimacy, it has certainly done so now. Poetica raises herself onto her knees and loyally, unflinchingly, inspects the injury, carefully teasing the area around the spot with the tip of her fingernail. Secundus flinches as she makes contact with the outer tip of the embedded sting.

"Alas, such sad soreness seems so sordid," she utters, immediately aware that, yet again, she has managed to skilfully do the business where the alliterative is concerned.

Across the room, the Fly is in kinks of laughter, doubled up as he surveys the fruits of the seed of disruption which he has venomously implanted. He knows that, in time, this little deed of vengeance will cause Secundus at least as equal a degree of discomfort as Administratus has had to endure in recent times, for – yes, indeed, you've been a witness to it – it is none other than our dear old pal, the Fly, which has caused Administratus' soreness also.

"Tee-hee!" the Fly says from behind the poker.

"Phwat was dat, Poetica?" asks Secundus, turning towards the fireplace.

"Alas, such sad soreness seems so sordid," she reiterates, revelling in her artistry.

"Jaysus, no, not dat. Dat noise. Did ya not hare some sskitter of a titter jussht now?"

"Not at all, loveen. You're just a little jittery at the minute, that's all. Come here to me, my little bundle," she says, lying back again and extending her open arms to him. Secundus' eyes widen and he beams as he looks down at her. Then, never a man to disappoint, he does as he is beckoned and the ould bit o' rolling and wrestling starts up once again and then, ho-ho … *deedle-diyddle-do*.

9
The Confluence of Things

Winter passes into Spring and, in no time at all, mid-April is upon the confraternity of Shapers and Rabble-Moracennans alike. The artistic workshop headed up by Secundus has, by now, gone into overdrive and back-to-back workshifts are the norm, such is the intent of Slagway's shapers to ensure that the Fresh Air parade will surpass all previous efforts. As for the Rabble-Moracennans, so clandestine are their activities and plans that, by this point, even yours truly, the teller of tall tales, great yarns and shaggy dog stories (*'Get the hell away from that mangey bitch there, Fido'*), is no longer privy to what may be going on at their headquarters. All that is known is that they have erected a newly set-up workshop out in the village of Nearba, where, it has been amicably agreed by both the Rabble and the Moracennans, city and country are deemed to have their meeting point.

Secundus is up the pole when Poetica enters the workshop. Since that night of smoke and steam, some three months back, they have not been together – he totally engrossed in readying for the upcoming parade, now a mere four months away, and she, as far as any knows, having been most industrious in adding a further two lines to whatever poem on which she had been working when last their paths (or whatever else you choose to mention) had crossed.

"Secundus," she beckons from the workshop floor, drawing the attention of the other workers to her. There is something in her tone of beckoning which Secundus, for some reason that he cannot fully identify to himself, does not like. He keeps his eyes fixed firmly on the work he is about.

"Secundus," she calls again, this time at a slightly higher pitch. He looks down, meets her eye and grimaces.

"Ah, Poetica, 'tish yarself dat's in it, ish it!" Then he slithers down the pole. His enthusiasm in descending from his perch is not quite what it was on that night of orgasmic fulfilment some months earlier. "So, den, how's it goin' wit ya?" he asks, as his feet touch the workshop floor.

"Can I speak with you in the office, Secundus?" Her tone of asking is somewhat serious.

"Aye, d'office, ish it? Aye, aye, to be shure ya can." He has tried not to show any sign of worry in his reply, but deep down he is fearful of what it is that he is about to hear. His fellow-workers in the building have momentarily stopped in their various doings of artistic endeavour and are gearing their attention towards Poetica and Secundus.

"Phwat d'ye tink yes are gawkin' at?" Secundus barks at them. "Jaysus, to look at ye, ya'd tink der was nuttin' to be done around dish plache."

"Nuttin'!" says one of the workers, fighting hard to conceal the grin that's mounting.

"Yeah, dat's what I said – nuttin'," retorts Secundus and, with that, the workers quickly avert their gazes back to their work again and Secundus and Poetica proceed towards the office.

Inside the office now they both are seated. The news for Secundus is not that good. Indeed, one might be forgiven for thinking that it isn't exactly the best bit of news Poetica herself has had in a long time either, but that is not entirely how she views it.

"Phwat! Prignunt!" he exclaims, repeating what she has just told him.

"Yes, Secundus, twins in fact."

"Twins! Jaysus, you mane der's more dan one of dem."

"Yes, Secundus, twins – two little babies."

"But, shure, didn't I only do it wit ya da onced? How could there be two of dem?"

Poetica, the more *composed*, has the wisdom to realise that now is not the time for lessons in the basics of biology. There are far more practical matters to be discussed at this point.

"Well, shure, we better see about gettin' the nechesshary done so, huh," says Secundus.

"The necessary, Secundus? And just what is it that you have in mind?"

"Arragh, ya know yarself. D'ould job, I mane."

"Job, Secundus?"

"Yeah, ya know, d'ould absorption."

Poetica looks aghast at this suggestion by Secundus that she should even think of ridding herself of her babies. It isn't, however – and God forbid that such might ever be the case – that she has any notion or desire that she and a mere second-in-command might get together in a common domicile. Indeed, the very idea of shared responsibility in this matter would be totally at variance with anything she has in mind.

"No, Secundus, you seem to miss the point."

"Missh da point! Missh da point, is it! Jaysus, 'tish an awful feckin' pity I didn't missh da friggin' point da night we war rollin' round d'effin' floor out dare. 'Tish all about misshin' points or hittin' points as far ash I can see." And as he makes this latter comment, yet another point of pertinence gains his attention. He raises one cheek of his arse from the chair and scratches that point which had been so scurrilously attacked by the Fly on that (now most ill-advised) night of nights. He is at a stage in his discomfort long since surpassed by his colleague Administratus and, unlike that selfsame cohort who is highly knowledgeable in matters of haute couture, he is not the proud possessor of any piece of apparel that is even remotely akin to a pair of silken, crimson brieffis.

"This is just the ticket I've been wishing for," Poetica announces.

"Ticket! Ticket, ish it? So, ya'r goin' ta have d'ould absorption after all!"

"What?"

"Ya know – over da water, I mane."

"No, Secundus, you silly man, not the right-to-travel-ticket. I'm speaking metaphorically. This is my ticket to security."

"Meta-phwat*ically*?"

"Metaphorically, Secundus."

Secundus is obviously bemused. "God knows, Poetica, but, do ya know phwat it ish: wit all dat ould language out o' ya, y'ar a hard woman ta undersshhtand at da bessht a times."

"Secundus, one little baby would have been so cherished

by the State – particularly in view of my prowess as a creator of high literature – that the weekly financial return, not to mention the various fringe benefits accruing, would have bettered my standard of living substantially. But now, Secundus, thanks to the marvellous strength and masculinity in your loins, I find myself not just artistically blessed, but also socially blessed on the double."

"Ya mane ya'r not goin' ta have the wee wans absorpted at all, at all?"

"That is exactly what I mean, Secundus."

Secundus holds his hands to his head and emits a long, forlorn sigh.

"But," Poetica now hastens to assure him, "there will be absolutely no implications or obligations in this matter for you, Secundus. None whatsoever."

Hands move from head now. The relief he feels on hearing this occasions a smile to creep out across his kisser. Whatsmore, though he does not yet know it, any second now, there is even better news to come.

"And, sure, I was thinking, Secundus, that, maybe in another couple of years, I might call around again of a drizzly winter's night when you might have occasion to stay back in the workshop to tighten up your nuts and we might see if you have the makings of another set of twins in your manly loins. Or, indeed, who knows – maybe triplets."

That smile which earlier had crept out across Secundus' kisser has now turned into a veritable beam and he can already feel a little stirring in the nether regions of his anatomy at the very thought of yet another visit to Poetica's holy of holies. He reaches across the desk and picks up his diary.

"Jussht let me have a gawk now," he says, feverishly thumbing the pages.

"No, no, Secundus, let's not plan it. We'll just ..." she pauses, "let it happen when it happens. What Maximus might term a *copulatus spontanatus*."

"Cop you'll ...! Right, right. Mighty, mighty," he exclaims. "But jussht one wee quesshtioneen, if ya don't mind me askin' now, Poetica: phwat's dis triplets crack dat ya minshunned jussht dare? Phwat classh of a yoke would ya be tinkin' of dare now?"

Poetica almost answers him, but then simply cocks her head and gazes west towards Nearba ...

In the Rabble-Moracennan workshop out in Nearba, all are as industrious as are those in the enemy camp in Slagway. Martineen and Stepheneen, accompanied by John James Joseph Michael Bartley Petereen, walk the workshop floor, stopping here and there to inspect the quality of the product being made by the Rabble-Moracennan machinists.

"Jaysus, der's a grate pint on dat altogedder, phwat!" says John James Joseph Michael Bartley Petereen, feeling the tip of the implement which he has just taken from one of the nearby Nearba machinists, then handing it to Stepheneen.

"Chrisht, mighty. Mighty!" and, as he says this, Stepheneen extends the implement on towards Martineen. The latter, however, unlike occasions of previous visitation to the workshop, shows little interest in the quality of the product. He dismissively diverts it from him by brushing it

aside with the back of his hand. Stepheneen and John
James Joseph Michael Bartley Petereen look at each other,
each knowing what it is that the other is thinking. Evidence
in recent weeks has suggested the growth of an aloofness
of sorts in Martineen's makeup. Some amongst the ranks
have even suggested the hitherto unthinkable: that there
are shades of the Shaper Administratus to be noticed in his
demeanour. In general, however, this suggestion has been
dismissed by a pointing to his use of language: not only has
his use of Rabble-babble remained faithfully as was, but he,
above all others of the new society, has been to the fore in
devoting time to the mastery of Garble.

"How many 'a dem have we made now?" asks
Martineen. His unexpected interest is welcome and serves
in its immediacy to dispel any doubt that his two
companions may have been feeling.

"God, der mussht be a tousshand of dem done by now,
Martineen," suggests John James Joseph Michael Bartley
Petereen, enthusiastically.

"A tousshand, begorrah!" remarks Martineen.

"Yera, no," says Stepheneen, scanning the piles of such
implements on the storage rails at the backs of the
machines. "Der's not a tousshand of dem done yet, and
dat's for shure."

"Well, tish well into da hundreds by now, at any rate,"
suggests John James Joseph Michael Bartley Petereen.

"Four hundred, maybe five, I'd say," says Stepheneen,
this time eyeing the piles at the machines that little bit more
carefully. "Five max, I'd say," he says. "Yeah, five max, at
the very mossht."

"Da word on da ground," says Martineneen, stopping

now and digging the point of his shoe into the workshop floor, "is that we will need a tousshand."

"A tousshand!" exclaims John James Joseph Michael Bartley Petereen.

"A tousshand," repeats Martineen, "dat's da word on da ground," and, this time, he makes more of a point of digging the toe of his shoe into the workshop floor.

His comrades look towards the floor and there, beside the tip of Martineen's shoe, written on the floor in a shade that is somewhere between scarlet and blood-drip red, is the magical figure of *1,000.*

"Ah, da word on da ground!" says Stepheneen, turning now to look at John James Joseph Michael Bartley Petereen.

"Ah!" says the latter. "Jaysus, boys, can't ye move a little fasshter on dem machines dare, phwat! God knows, da month of Augussht will be on top of us before we notice September is gone."

"But, John James Joseph Michael Bartley Petereen," begins one of the nearby machinists, thinking, in his innocence, to provide a little elucidation on the nature of calendrical sequence, "Augussht comes bef–"

"Ah here, for the love and honour of God," barks John James Joseph Michael Bartley Petereen, "none o' dat ould American bullshit about Augussht comin' before da Fall outa ya. Jaysus, der's nexxht to nuttin' done and, God knows, if it sshtays like dis der'll be even less done dan what's been done up to now."

The machinists, bewildered, look at one another, trying to figure out exactly what it is that John James Joseph Michael Bartley Petereen's words have actually meant, not suspecting for a second that an even greater challenge in verbosity is about to be released.

"Come on, come on, da lot of ye, back to work, back to work. Come on now, lads, sshpread yarselves out in a bunch dare, will ye!"

10

A Jolt of Jealousy and the Threat of Treachery Most Foul

Early May. Administratus' debilitation of recent months has seen him play a less industrious role than would have usually been the case in previous years. Still, so splendidly successful were proceedings that 'Night of the Rreadink' – now several months back – that the mere memory of it, coupled with occasional mention by some sycophant or other, has been sufficient to keep his sense of self importance – of indispensability, indeed – at a reasonably high level. It is just some such mention that occupies his mind as he sits alone in the doctor's waiting room. Indeed, so mesmeric is the memory that Secundus' coming into the room goes unnoticed by him.

"'Tish yarself so, Y-J," says Secundus, by way of greeting his more elegant comrade.

Administratus turns his head. It is the class of a head-turn that only he can successfully effect.

"Ah, Secundus, my good man! Yes, yes indeed, I do believe you are right."

"Phwat?" asks Secundus, already bemused by Administratus' first venture into conversation.

"You are right, I say: it *is* myself."

Jaysus, thinks poor ould Secundus to himself, 'dis could

be a bitteen of a rough sittin'. Better to keep it fairly simple', he decides.

" 'Tish a grate ould bitta wedder we're gittin' dish passht while, phwat! All dat sunshine and all, ya know."

This time Administratus' turn of the head is of a different variety. Though of equal class and elegance to the earlier turn, this one carries with it the extra ingredient of disdain towards his comrade. Its causticity is added to by the fact that not a single word accompanies the head-turn. The subsequent moments of silence prove too much for Secundus and something deep within him compels him to foolishly venture into the world of speech again.

"Ish it ta see himself ya'r here?" he asks, nodding towards the soothing jade-coloured door on which the brass plate bearing the name of Shaperus Doctorus is mounted. One could well be forgiven for thinking that Secundus is intent on inviting one rebuke after another.

"No, Secundus, I am here to purchase a new car."

Secundus' state of bewilderment is going from bad to worse as he tries to figure this one out.

"A new car! Be da japers, and I never knowed he did cars as well as d'ould bitta doctorin' sshtuff. Begorrah and dat's a quare wan all right," and now Secundus looks all the more closely at the brass plate on the office door, then back towards Administratus once again. The latter has kept his profile towards the other and Secundus can tell from his comrade's demeanour that there has been some cryptic Y-J dimension in this reference by Administratus to car purchase – a dimension which Secundus can do no better than acknowledge to himself as being simply way above him.

"Ah, right! Got ya," and, as he says this, he winks at Administratus' profile. Then they both sit in silence, one uncomfortable with his inability to think of something he might say that might merit a creditable answer from his comrade, the other smugly confident of the righteousness of his decision to treat his associate with disdain. The level of discomfort so mounts for Secundus that, when finally he yields to the mental pressure and makes comment once again, he is delectably surprised to find that what he has to say is deemed of interest to Administratus.

"I hare der's right feverish work goin' on beyond in Nearba."

"Is that so?" replies Administratus, and this time, the fact that there is some level of interest in the matter to him keeps him from looking so disdainfully at his fellow-shaper. "And what class of work would we be talking of, Secundus?"

"Jaysus, I don't know for shure now, like. All's I knows is that der's a fierche mountain o' sshmoke supposed ta be climbin' up outa d'ould chimbley out dare where dey builded dat new plache o' dares. Jay, someone was tellin' me jussht d'udder day dat the sshmoke is so grey betimes dat it's black."

"Hmm! Sounds almost papal."

"Phwat?"

"Sounds almost papal, I said, Secundus."

"Naw, naw, not purple. A heavy grey to black is phwat dey was sayin'."

"Hmm!"

The likelihood of yet another prolonged pause is suddenly banished by the unexpected opening of Shaperus

Doctorus' door.

"Very good, very good, Master Maximus," Doctorus is heard to say and then both he and Maximus, most noble of most noble shapers, emerge into the waiting room.

Administratus and Secundus both sit upright, then each tries inconspicuously to lean forward a little so as to catch the attention of the Mighty Maximus.

"Just spray …" – Doctorus pauses, takes cognisance of the persons seated in the waiting room – "just spray the affected area twice daily, Maximus, once in the morning and once at night, and avoid any further exposure. Spring's nearly at an end and, as you know all too well, they'll be flying all over the place again throughout the summer months." Then Shaperus Doctorus winks at Maximus, knowing that his coded message has been understood. Maximus raises his index finger and twice gently taps the side of his nose, indicating to his Hippocratic friend that, for all that may or may not be said about the classiness of nods, the wink just given has most certainly been as good as the very best of them.

"Quite," the pillar of the Arts says, shakes hands with Shaperus Doctorus and, not gracing either of the seated shapers with so much as a fleeting glance, quickly departs the scene.

Doctorus turns, his morning's work made so much more worthwhile by his having been of service to the unequalled Maximus. "Ah," he says, on seeing Administratus and Secundus, the enthusiasm of his tone dipping somewhat at the prospect now of having to be of service to shapers of a lesser calibre than he who has just left the office. "Whichever of you is next."

Doctorus has proceeded back into his office, but Secundus and Administratus sit, mouths agape, looking at each other. Though nothing of its nature has been spoken, each has intuitively understood the other's complaint and, worse again by far, that same intuition has made them realise that the ailment which has brought them to Doctorus' office is the very ailment which has also occasioned Maximus to have presented himself on the day: an ailment visited upon all three in similar, if not identical, circumstances – no one of the three having been able, on the occasion when the stinging injury was dealt, to resist the favours offered by the peccadillian poetic promptress.

"Poetica!" the boys exclaim in unison. "The slovenly, syllabic slut!"

"Next, please," calls Doctorus from the room within, and he too now, unseen by the two outside, raises a cheek and has a private little scratch ...

Out in Nearba, Martineen has finally succeeded in reaching his office and is now ensconced in the wine-red, leatherette-upholstered executive chair which has been especially acquired for him. Though he has said nothing of it, it has, in no small way, annoyed him that, amongst the rank and file of both the Rabble and the Moracennans, his commitment to the cause of overthrowing the Shapers is being called into question. That John James Joseph Michael Bartley Petereen and, worse again, Stepheneen – a Rabble kinsman of his own – could possibly think him disloyal is an even greater blow. Still, he, in his own heart, knows he is no traitor and that, he feels sure, will become increasingly evident to one and all as the great August parade of the Shapers approaches. But Martineen, confident and all as he is, cannot know what may happen between now and the highlight of the summer.

His mind now is distracted by the buzzing of a fly. He leans forward in his seat, raises his folded copy of THE OIRISH CHIMES from the desk, thinks momentarily of the now well-gone Duwell, then swipes at the winged creature as it crosses his line of vision. He has learned, since recently he has begun to purchase the CHIMES, that, in the whole of the Western world, there is no commercially made fly swatter better than the said publication.

"Drat, misshed da hoorin' little fecker," he says, then slumps back into the chair and tosses the CHIMES onto the desk again.

Just as well that he has missed, indeed, for this fly is none of your commoner garden variety of fly. This here is our ubiquitous friend of yore, augurer and oft-times overseer of important happenings and, as such, fully deserving of that capital letter that distinguishes him from all other flies: he is, of course, the Fly. He is now safely concealed on the inside of the shade of the brass reading lamp on Martineen's desk, perfectly positioned to take in the major part of the leading article of the CHIMES. It is a piece about the prospective drying up of European funds for the Arts and is occupying the Fly's little mind when Martineen's phone rings.

"Halo," says Martineen, some seconds before he actually manages to get the receiver to his mouth.

"Hellew," he says then, realising that his first effort has been missed by the caller and taking advantage of the fortuitous opportunity offered by the intervening seconds to modify his tone of speech somewhat … 'Oh-oh,' thinks the Fly, 'maybe the boys are right. Maybe the little shagger *is* beginning to lose the run of himself.'

"Hello, Martineen – you don't mind, I hope, if I call you by your first name. This is Poetica, the great maker of lays in Slagway."

The Fly has heard the introduction and takes immediate stock of the fact that Martineen has sat upright in his seat and is straightening his collar.

"P-P-P-Poetica, the Poet. No, no, not at all. Martineen is fine, fine. Shure, haven't we got some friends, or, at leasht, acquaintances in common."

"Yes, quite."

"And shure, when I tink of it, like, didn't we often have a drink in da same company, even if we never acchually met each other."

"Indeed, Martineen, and that is precisely why I am phoning you."

"I beg yar pardon?"

"I thought that we might meet – over a drink, that is. It seems a shame that two such luminaries as we should not have met person-to-person before now."

The irrepressible Fly smells a rat immediately and is alarmed to see from Martineen's beaming countenance that the greatest fears of disloyalty and betrayal seem potentially not so incorrect.

"Where, when and as soon as possible, plase," says Martineen in one flowing gush of naivety and over-eagerness.

'Well, ya feckin' fool', thinks the Fly. 'Ya Poor,

Unfortunate, Gullible, Unthinking Gobshite – ya PUGUG ya.'

"Well, at the moment I'm with my pleasantly palindromic publisher, ANCICNA, out here past Nearba, but I will be returning to Slagway later. Perhaps somewhere convenient for both of us?"

"Pass da problem," says Martineen, "pass da problem at all at all."

The Fly crosses his forelegs and squirms on hearing this barbarous and savage malapropism of language. Bear in mind that he, by virtue of his grandfather's status as an African tsetse who lived much of his winged life in French-occupied Algeria, has inherited his forebearer's knowledge of that exquisite Gallic tongue.

"I'm sorry, Martineen, I don't quite understand," Poetica tells the Slagwayan.

"Pass da problem – no problem, like, ya know what I mean. Jaysus, sorry about dat now, Poetica. I'da shworn ya spoke d'ould bitta German."

"German, Martineen? No – no, I don't, not on Tuesdays at any rate. Apropos our meeting, I gather Knocked Down's would be out of the question?"

"Apro– wat? Ah, ya'r a right ould cod altogedder. Ya do spake d'ould German after all. But, God, no – not Knocked Down's. Jaysus, dat'd get me in right trouble like, ya know. Couldn't mate ya in The Locks aither. Too dicey, ya know what I mane like."

"Well, how about my apa*w*rtment then?"

"Where's dat? Is dat da new pub in town?"

"No, no, Martineen, my apa*w*rtment – where I live. Perhaps we could have drinkies and discuss things there.

Come to think of it, it would be far more private than any of the other options."

"Yar own place?" says Martineen, and he runs the back of his hand inside the collar of his shirt to wipe away the mounting sweat. "Fine," says he, the utterance several octaves higher than the usual pitch of his voice. "Fine," he says a second time, this time quite deeply so as to deliberately emphasise his masculinity.

"Good. The address is 99 rue des Écrivains, Apa*w*rtment P. Shall we say sixish?"

The Fly oversees the writing of Poetica's address on the blotting pad on Martineen's desk. It is an address with which our aerial friend is quite familiar, for it was there that he had occasion to have dealt respective stings to the buttocks of both Maximus and Administratus – the little infliction to Secundus' fleshy part being the exception in that Poetica was, most uncharacteristically, playing away from home on that occasion.

All of which takes us back to where we came into this chapter on the bawdy lives of the high and low of Slagway – a fitting time for this scribe to shift his tent elsewhere and see what else is going on in the environs of everybody's favourite place …

11

Obsession and Confession, then a little more Obsession

June, she'll change her tune/ In restless walks she'll prowl the night/ July, she will fly/ And give no warning to her flight/ August, die she must/ The autumn winds blow chilly and cold …

"Ahhh!" screams Administratus, and he bolts upright in his bed, sweat teeming from his brow and his heart palpitating at an alarming rate. The darkness of his room prevents him from immediately identifying anything that is around him. Eventually, his eyes locate the garish red numbers of the electric digital clock to one side of his bed: 3.33am. He sits pertly erect, presses his back hard against the headboard and draws several deep breaths. He reaches out to the bedside locker, feels around and locates his lighter and his pack of Camel cigarettes. He opens, picks, lights and, within seconds, he is drawing heavily on the burning weed.

More composed now, he begins to try to make sense of his nightmare. Christ, if any of the more illustrious shapers was ever to learn that he, Administratus, had dreamt of and, worse again, could actually recall verbatim the words of any Paul & Arty ditty, his reputation would be well and truly funkeled. Another glance at the face of the clock confirms for him that his awakening has, at least, coincided with the mention in the song of the current month. The top right-hand corner of the clockface tells him that it is, indeed, the month of August and, even more precisely, August 15 – the day of the big parade – when Secundus' and his workers' efforts to artistically depict the Fresh Air Theme will be laid bare before the whole of the Slagwayan world.

The more he smokes, the more alert his mind becomes and the better he is able to make sense of what, at first, seemed an incomprehensible dream … *'June, she'll change her tune, in restless walks she'll prowl the night'* – this, beyond all question, is his subconscious concern about what the world and his mother now know to be the obnoxious and publicly open affair being conducted between Poetica and that semi-Rabbleian guttersnipe, Martineen. Martineen, whom, Administratus now remembers, dared, one night in Knocked Down's, to presume to introduce him to Duwell of the *CHIMES*.

Another drag on his dromedary fag and Administratus' mind flits to the next line of the song: *'July, she will fly and give no warning to her flight'*. As he recalls it, he has the visual image of there being an emphasis on the word 'fly'. A simpler mind might think the line to be a reference to Poetica's flightiness, but Administratus, dutifully daily doer of the *CHIMES*' cryptic crossword, knows that the deeper importance of the clue is in the word 'fly'. As though inspired now, the memory of having seen the degenerate Martineen on a number of occasions recently busily scratching his arse as he travelled the narrow streets of Slagway, suddenly helps the forming realisation to come to fruition in his mind. Christ! Martineen, much more of Rabble than of Shaper form! He, too, just like himself, like Maximus, like Secundus, has been stung by the Fly!!! And the common thread? Poetica, the bitch. Huh, he thinks, a very common thread, indeed.

The realisation prompts a reaching for the bedside lamp and soon the light it sheds is cast upon our hero's furrowed brow. The little bitch, he thinks again, and she supposed to be so busily engaged in the completion of her collection. Huh, collection how are you! A collection of lays right enough and of that there can be no mistake. But why this sudden reckless abandon on her part, he wonders? Of course, he can readily understand how she would have wanted to have had her way with *him*: the very fact that the light cast by the bedside lamp allows him see himself in the mirror on the wall at the end of the bed is explanation enough of why she would have naturally desired him. And, of course, the esteemed Maximus: that he can also understand. Even Secundus, too, can almost, at this stage, gain near acceptability in his mind. But Martineen! My God, my God, my God!

He eases back the quilt, swivels gingerly into a seated position on the edge of the bed, locates his crimson velvet slippers without looking, then stands out bollock-naked on the floor. He moves directly to the mirror now, stands for several seconds to admire himself in his entirety and then locates his dressing gown and heads out for the kitchen.

In the kitchen now, the fag in one hand and the coffee mug in the other. His mind is focusing on the final Simon & Garfunkel line: '*August, die she must. The autumn winds blow chilly and cold*'. Die she must, he thinks. Is it Poetica?

Surely not. She is as hale and hearty-looking as ever. No, no, never the simple explanation for our Administratus. There is, unquestionably, a hidden meaning in this line also. Yes, there is, and whatsmore, it is his intellectual duty to find it, for it is, he feels sure now, a prognostication of some sort or other, and one, he equally strongly feels, that may have major implications for what is soon to come.

'August, die she must. The autumn winds blow chilly and cold'. Christ, this time Administratus finds himself actually singing the line and, worse again, he is giving it the undue reverence of delivering it in tune. He slaps his hand on to his mouth lest any further words should involuntarily make their way out into the world of listendom. He reddens, thinks immediately of that night of the Rreadink when he so carelessly uttered the word 'fuck' as 'fuck' instead of the much more elegant 'ffock'. He looks around – just as he had done on that occasion – and checks that there is no one behind him. In his own kitchen! At three-thirty something in the morning! Christ, he thinks, that dream has really shaken me up a bit.

He raises the cup of coffee and is just about to sip when the phone rings. The start it occasions causes him to jolt and to spill some of the coffee onto his coveted dressing gown. Just one ring of the phone, then silence again. Jesus, he thinks, they're watching me, then this is quickly followed by the thought that he is becoming paranoid. Another sip of coffee, a rationalising of the situation and an understanding that all of this lack of composure is simply the after-effect of the horrendous nightmare that he has had.

"Bollocks," he says, throws back the coffee and heads off to bed again. Of course, I, the writer, and you, the reader,

understanding our dear Administratus as we do, really
know that what he had meant to say was 'Testicles'.

"Uhhhhhh," groans Martineen, as he rolls himself off
the body that lies beneath him in Apawrtment P at 99 rue
des Écrivains. "Jaysus, d'ya know wat it is but I'm only
knackered, but dat was grate altogedder all da same," says
he.

"Quite," responds Poetica.

Martineen is oblivious to the fact that her comment on
the performance is considerably less enthusiastic than is
his. Her mind, if truth were known, is elsewhere. As
Martineen lies on his back, still panting from the effort, his
eyes focus on a black speck above them on the ceiling. For
a second or two he thinks he has seen it moving, but then
he comes to think that it is his eyes playing tricks on him.
Sure, how could any man's faculties be functioning on full
voltage after the energy he has just spent, he thinks.

"Dat's an ugly ould bit of a sshpeck ya have up dare on
da ceilin', Poetica."

"What?" she asks, drawing on the Gauloise she has lit
while Martineen was preoccupied with identifying for
himself how thoroughly satisfied he has been.

"Dat sshpeck dare," says he, this time pointing towards
the spot. Her eyes follow his direction and then she
chidingly tells him: "For God's sake, Martineen, that's not
a speck – it's a common run-of-the-mill housefly."

Overhead, the insect arches his back in anger at hearing
his status so diminished, and, as he does so, Martineen
spots the movement.

"Musha, do ya know wat it is, but yar dead right – 'tis only an ould fly."

"*Tee-hee,*" says the Fly, loudly enough that it is heard below in the bed.

"What did you say?" asks Poetica, it immediately registering with her that the night she and Secundus had turned steam to water, then back to steam again, he too had said something of having heard exactly what she has just heard.

"I said, musha, do ya know wat –"

"No, no, after that, after that!"

"Jaysus, and I didn't say nuttin' at all after dat."

"No, Martineen, I distinctly heard you say something silly like 'Tee-hee'."

"Wat! Sure washn't it you who said 'Tee-hee'?"

They turn their heads on their respective pillows and look over at each other, and each can tell that the other is deadly serious in what has been said.

"But –," they both say together, then stop and turn their gazes towards the ceiling.

"Tee-hee, tee-hee," says the Fly, and he eases himself away from the plane of white above and conceals himself elsewhere in the room. The two below turn towards each other yet again, simultaneously take hold of the top of the quilt and gently draw it up to shoulder level so as to protect their modesty.

It is quite some time before either Martineen or Poetica speak again and finally it is she who breaks the silence.

"How are you feeling now, then, Martineen?"

"Yerra, I'm grand, grand, grand."

"You know the day that's in it, don't you?"

"Do I wat! Of course I do. Shure ishn't it everythin' I've been workin' towards since first ever I realised dat dem shapers never had a whit a' time for me. Too feckin' good for me day tought day was. Bejaysus, and I'll show dem before da day is out wat it manes ta be a rale Slagwayan. So help me God, I will."

The passion in his speech excites Poetica and subconsciously prompts her to trust her man a little more. She nestles into him and lowers her hand down beneath the quilt to touch his – kneecap.

"Martineen."

"Yes, loveen?"

"Do you remember you asked me when first we got together why, after my long association with them, I suddenly wanted to join in the conspiracy against the shapers?"

"Yes, luv." He loves how she has come to embrace his ideology and always feels that that espousal is never better evidenced than when she, the great Poetica, so effortlessly refers to her ex-cohorts as shapers. He turns in towards her, sensing that there is something in the offing that he hasn't heard before.

"And do you remember what it was that I told you?"

"Of course I do, Poetica. It was dat ya had suddenly come to da ralisashun dat da rale paple of Slagway was bein' excl... excl... excl..."

"Excluded, love, excluded."

"Yeah, dat's it. Dat dey was bein' excluded from d'Arts and dat dat should be changed."

"Yes, Martineen, my lover, and so it should be. But I wasn't being entirely honest with you at the time."

Whether strategically or otherwise, Poetica begins to sob, quickly going from slight to bitter sobbing, and Martineen, great man of the Rabble and the Rabble-Moracennans that he has become, draws her even closer to console her.

"Ah here, luv, wat is it at all at all at all at all dat's atin' at ya, wat?"

Sensing she has already won him over, she sobs a little harder again before speaking. "The straw that broke the camel's back for me was —" Again, the theatrically well-timed pause sucks him in even more. "Was —" Yet another pause.

"Come on, Poetica, luv, don't ya know I'm here for ya and dat no matter wat it was dat caused ya ta change yar mind, shure 'n I'll undershtand, huh?"

"You're so good, so understanding, so … manly, my Martineen."

Martineen's ego is swelling and again he encourages her to share her little secret with him.

"It was Maximus," she says, in something of a whimper. "Wat?"

"Maximus," she tells Martineen a second time.

"Wat d'ya mane 'it was Maximus'?"

"It was Maximus who made me switch allegiance. You see, he and I were – well, how best can I put it – occasional lovers."

Poetica sees jealousy in all its greenness rise in Martineen's eyes. Seed number one is sewn and she knows she's on a winner.

"Not lovers like you and I are, Martineen. No one could possibly be like you," she quickly adds, noticing that this functions well to quell any danger of his anger overflowing. "You see, Maximus and I had, over the years, had the odd little fling. He had always suspected that I was limited as a poet and, in time, there were things he learned about my practice of the art which he came to hold over me."

"Wat?"

"Little irregularities, one might term them."

"Irregurrallities! But, couldn't ya jussht have told him ta feck off da hell wit himself?"

"Well, it wasn't quite that easy, Martineen. You see, his suspicions were …" she pauses, "correct."

Martineen's eyes widen. He sits upright in the bed and looks at her. "Wat?"

"Yes, Martineen, I'm afraid it's true." She has gambled in telling him all of this, but her judgement of the situation, since earlier seeing the green-eyed monster in Martineen's stare, is that she is still on course to keep favour with him.

"But wat about all dem grate pomes ya've written over da years, like, huh? Wat about dem?"

"All forgeries, Martineen. Pieces borrowed here and there, some rearranged a little and some not even that."

"But shure, washn't some a' dem published, like, wit yar name on dem and all? Shure, ya'r not goin' ta tell me dat dat grate pome about poor ould Duwell was stolen from somewhere or udder?"

She sobs heavily again, a slight nodding of her head, then, "An ill-disguised version of an elegy found in a book of English verse, I'm afraid."

Martineen might well be feeling as shattered as he is amazed except that now he realises that he himself is in an even stronger position than ever. Where previously he has been in awe of Poetica's prowess, he suddenly realises that now his hand is considerably stronger than ever it has been before.

"Maximus upped the anti considerably, Martineen, and expected me to be there for him at his beck and call, whenever the humour would come over him for a little bit of the how's yar father."

"Well, da hoorin' bollocks, and him a FART and all," exclaims Martineen.

"He told me that if I refused to co-operate, he would let the cat out of the bag and expose me as a fraud."

"Jaysus, he was goin' ta set a cat on ya, wat!"

"No, no, Martineen, I meant that metaphorica–" She pauses a second, remembering the confusion that ensued when last she used the term. "It's only a figure of speech."

"Bejapers! Maximus!"

"Yes," whimpers Poetica, and then she bursts into a full flood of tears, intermingling their shedding with an abiding and occasional sob, giving total authenticity to the degree of her upset.

"Y'ar all right, loveen. Me and you is a team and we'll show Maximus and his crew wat's feckinwell wat before da day is out."

"Oh, Martineen, my Martineen," she says, as she turns back into him, twirls his kneecap a little and a wee bitteen of a rattle and hum starts up again. Oh, ohh, ohhhhhh – the hills are alive with the sound of music …

"Tee-hee," says the Fly – this time unheard – and, armed now with Coke and popcorn, he reassumes his position overhead and settles in to watch the next performance.

"What's that, what's that?" screams Administratus, shooting upright in his bed again on the other side of town. "I thought I heard a feckin' fly," he mutters to himself, then comes to the conclusion that it is only his imagination playing tricks on him again.

"*Tee-hee*."

12

Hubble, Bubble, Toil and Brewing Trouble

"Aisey, aisey on now, will ye. Jaysus, will ye watch de feckin' metal girder," barks Secundus, as he points overhead to where much of what is now being rolled out under wraps has originally been constructed. In less stressed times, his fonder memory of that very girder would be that that is where he had stood straddle-legged on that night of nights when he and Poetica had finally managed to get screw and nut together. But, right now, his undivided attention is given to the work in hand.

"Aisey now, boys and girrels, dat's it, nice and aisey does it."

Under his tutelage, or, perhaps more pertinently, despite his tutelage, the workers succeed in moving the covered display towards the workshop's double doors. A huge green canvas tarpaulin covers it and nothing is visible other than the gigantic wheels of the transport frame upon which the display has been mounted. The Fresh Air Theme sits in all its glory beneath the weighty sheet and, in a small few hours, the product of yet another nine months' artistic endeavour will be unveiled, not just before the denizens of the city, but also before the throngs who annually make the pilgrimage to Slagway – their artistic Mecca – in their thousands to witness the phenomenal event.

"Now den, gadder in here around me and sshpread out a bitteen, will ye," instructs Secundus.

Much bumping of one into the other ensues. His workers – mere minnows of the world of shaperdom and amongst whom indecision is already more the norm than an occasional interloper – endeavour, at one and the same time, to comply with both elements of his instruction. They know what is to come. Some of their number have been there in previous years and have come to realise that, on this morning every year, the Fund for Artistic Endeavour in Slagway (commonly known as FAES) generously stretches the elasticity of its purse strings to veritable breaking point and, in anticipation of the hard day's work that lies ahead, makes available to the workers a pre-celebratory imbibition of the native Slagway grog known as *Tóipín*.

The eyes of those gathered flit fleetingly from one to the other in their stares, some in curious anticipation of their first taste of the illicit potion, others – the more bleary-eyed – in naked need of the cure that it may offer in the wake of the activities of the night before.

All eyes suddenly become centrally refocused on the towering Secundus as he unexpectedly explodes into a ritualistic rendition of the ancient single-lined 'Invocation of the Tóipín':

"*Raihbat acham na béist,*" he sings.

Though none in the attendance is absolutely sure of its literal translation, it has been mooted on previous occasions that it is the equivalent of 'Bring on the Beast', the beast in question presumably being the Tóipín.

On a western hillside overlooking Slagway, halfway

between that city's perimeter and the village of Nearba, Martineen the brave has, at the very same second as has Secundus, issued from the depth of his lungs the cry of '*Raihbat acham na béist*'.

His cry, just like that of Secundus, is followed by the hasty rolling forth of a mighty cast-iron cauldron from which an aromatic steam is rising. To either side of Martineen stands his own man, Stepheneen and the staunch and rugged John James Joseph Michael Bartley Petereen. The men and women in the Rabble-Moracennan ranks immediately divest themselves of the shafted implements they have carried to this point and hastily gather around the cauldron. Their brotherhood lacking official recognition, and thereby unable to draw on the FAES Fund, the contents of the Rabble-Moracennan cauldron has been paid for out of their own coffers. An attendant comes forward and extends a silver ladle to Martineen. Their leader takes, he dips, he lifts, he tastes.

"Ara," he cries, "át és og fucking tionhach".

His followers roar in delirious appreciation. It is his first ever public utterance in the hybrid tongue of the Rabble-Moracennans and never could any occasion befit such an utterance as this, the day when the degradation dealt out by the shapers for years uncounted would finally be avenged.

Martineen now lowers the ladle from his lips. "Og tinnce, át és og amith." More cheering from the gathering on hearing his pronouncement that yes, most definitely, the Tóipín has met with his approval.

A ritual passing of the ladle by Martineen to John James Joseph Michael Bartley Petereen. The latter raises the silver utensil to his lips, the sun catching the brightness of the

precious metal as he does so. He sips at first, eases the ladle
from his lips momentarily and then, full-bloodedly, throws
back its contents in one awesome swallow. His eyes redden
with the fire of battle-in-prospect and, as he exhales, his
breath is of a visibly blue hue against the distant city
skyline. The Fly, untimely hovering in the line of exhalation,
spirals in the pungency of the breath-created mist and is
inexplicably jettisoned at phenomenal speed in the direction
of Slagway.

"Ír-bhaltsa ra daf, a chaolra," John James Joseph Michael
Bartley Petereen tells the assembly, reiterating the sentiment
of Martineen's judgement on the Tóipín.

More shouting and rejoicing, then a sudden surging
forth by all and sundry, and some hours will be spent
reducing the liquid level from cauldron's top to bottom.

Back in Slagway, the members of Secundus' motley crew
have already considerably lowered their own cauldron's
level. A breeze sweeps in the double doors of the city
workshop, carrying with it none other than the Fly. He is
swept towards the cauldron and now, above it, he spirals
once again, but this time in a tailspin. Frantic flapping of
his wings to keep him from immersion in the steaming
brew, a stretching of his legs, a closing of one eye and then,
just as he is about to meet his Tóipínloo, he is miraculously
and totally unintentionally saved by some insignificant serf
of shaperdom who has stepped forward for a refill and
accidentally catches our intrepid friend in his empty glass.

"Jaysus, feckin' flies is everywhere dis wedder," he
comments disgruntedly, and proceeds to toss our little

bugger out of the glass. He is flung across the room and, as luck would have it, comes to rest in the softest of soft landing places: where else, indeed, but nestled warmly in Poetica's deep cleavage, snugly pressed on either side by the cosy voluptuousness of her breasts. He is surprised to find himself so intimately close, perhaps, but not really that surprised to see Poetica in attendance. After all, he had, earlier that morning, from his aerial-ringside seat, heard Martineen's discussion with her and was privy to their decision that she should show her face (not to mention anything else) at the shapers' workshop. That way, even the tiniest suspicion that she might be part of any conspiracy would be totally avoided.

"Poetica, me girreleen-o," booms Secundus as he spots her across the workshop floor. He makes for her and, as he does, the Fly decides to forego his pleasurable comfort and zooms upwards to one of the rafters overhead.

"So, den, how's da little ones doin' at all at all?" the cumbersome artificer asks, as he places his shovel of a hand against her navel. She looks as shapely as ever, so much so, indeed, that even Martineen, despite the intimacy between them, had suspected nothing of her condition and it is only this very morning, after several little rolls (i.e. rolleens) in the hay that she has confided her secret in him. It must be said, however, that, in telling him of her circumstances, she so constructed the story that Martineen felt all the more compelled to avenge the insult given to his prized one.

"I was tinkin' about dat little suggeschun ya had wan a' da lassht times we was sshpakin," says Secundus.

"Suggestion? And just what suggestion was that, Secundus?"

"Ya know, da wan ya was sayin about how mebbe yarself and meself 'd git togedder agin some time and give it an ould blassht for da giblets."

"Giblets?"

"Yeah, ya know," he says, making three little gyrating thrusts of his pelvis towards her.

"Oh, you mean triplets! No, Secundus, I don't th—" And then she stops herself. "Well, actually, that might not be a bad idea, dearie," and, as she utters the measured little endearment, she draws a wee bit closer to him and allows him drool a little over her bountiful endowment. The prospect of what is to happen on this day of days has so enthused her that an extra little conning of the fool is irresistible to her.

"Oh, Jaysus, God knows and I'm not a well man at all at all," he says, wiping sweat from his brow and visibly shuddering from head to toe.

"Later, sweetie, after the parade, when all decent Slagwayans have homeward gone."

His eyes are globular as they feast upon her curvaceousness and the prospect of him, yet again, having his way with her is straining the lips of his eye sockets to the limit to contain his ocular blue balls.

"Now, be a darling and get me another little glassheen of the Tóipín, will you?"

He takes her glass and eagerly begins to head back towards the cauldron.

"*Tee-hee.*"

Secundus stops and looks back towards Poetica.

"Phwat was dat, huh?"

"What was what, my precious?" she asks, lasciviously

pursing her lips at the utterance of yet another alluring pronouncement and totally beguiling him so that neither his own 'Phwat was dat?' or her 'What was what?' matters any longer.

"I'll git da drink," says he, and he dutifully bounds off towards the Tóipín.

13

Pricks and Prods and Oh my Gods and then the Bubble bursts

Midday. The crowds have converged on the city. Those more favoured have managed to gain position in the Square where proceedings will commence and whence this year's parade on the much awaited Fresh Air Theme will depart along its oh so merry way.

Those less fortunate, realising that the opportunity to take up a vantage point in the environs of the Square is gone, have taken themselves towards the harbour wall and dockland area where, as long years of attendance has informed them, the parade will come to a spectacular conclusion later in the afternoon: who knows, maybe even more spectacular than anticipated this particular year!

The least favoured of all have already lined the sidewalks along the myriad of streets through which Secundus will lead his now half-tanked crew. Some time later, these unsuspecting patrons will generously applaud as the shaperly minnows hoist this year's astonishing offering on poles of, what columnists in the *Atomiser* and *Turbine* have already reliably informed them to be, specially reinforced Sheffield steel.

Alas now, back at the Square, there is a stir of excitement amongst those gathered. All eyes focus on the area at the western side of the city's focal point where the platform, from which the dignitaries will speak, has been erected. There is a drone of expectation, and then the audible communal sigh of the many gathered, as an eminent line of cap-and-cape bedecked fathers of the city is seen to bob and weave its way in the direction of the platform.

Those in the populist assembly stretch and strain their necks in an effort to identify these elders, many of the opinion that the more of their number that they can identify, then the greater their own importance in the eyes of the socialites they so admire. All stretching, straining, striving is dismissed for nothing when the notables begin to mount the steps at one side of the platform. Now, even the most common of plebs can see them clearly and there is not quite the same degree of kudos going with any claim of being able to name one beyond the other. The big wigs sit.

A hush. The Mayor of Slagway stands and comes forward to the microphone. He is beloved of a few in the assembly – very few. Indeed, for the most part, those in the gathering are unable to say whether he is an eFFin' Gee'r or an eFFin' eFFer, or indeed, even a one-time red but now a putridly paling pink and lily-livered labouring eFFer. On this day of days, such status has finally found its common level of non-important sameness. The din amongst the crowd raises once again and the few words the mayor chooses to say go thankfully unnoticed. It is only now, as the members of the crowd see brave Maximus approach the mic, that the silence is restored. Most cherished by the denizens, regardless of the eFFin' hue, he is distinctly and distinguishedly greyer than he had been when last the common people would have seen him.

Maximus takes time to peruse the crowd before commencing. Despite his scanning of their number, the weaving in their midst of Martineen and Stepheneen – each at opposite sides of the Square – goes unnoticed by him. Each is hooded, a relatively inconspicuous choice of attire given the day that's in it, and each carries beneath his cloak the twin assets of a sharply pointed spear and a mobile phone. Indeed, the decision to carry the latter on the day has been hard-won as it has only come about after lecherous allegations by some in the Rabble-Moracennan ranks that such would be little more than a treacherous act of shaperdom and a blatant betrayal of all that their recently founded brotherhood purports to hold sacred. A vote on the matter has decided the issue by the slim margin of one – and that itself only with a rider that use of the unmentionable gadget will, after this day's activities are done, be abandoned for ever after. Once in position, both Martineen and Stepheneen lower their hoods and look towards the platform.

"People of Slagway, people of the Aesthetic, people of Artdom," begins Maximus, then he is marvellously interrupted by the discerning wildness of applause which his opening occasions amongst his listeners. Then calm reigns once again.

"This is a great day. This is the day that you and I have eagerly awaited. Tradition suggests the wonders to which we can look forward. Years of splendiferous creation has raised our expectations of what we may witness on this day every year. But, my friends, appetites for the spectacular have never been so keen and, having heard, through the grapevine, of the sensational nature of this year's parade, I can assure you that you will not be disappointed. The Fresh Air Theme is, dare I say it, by far the most daring and most enterprising undertaken by Shaperus Secundus and his troop. Those cognoscenti who have been privileged to have had a preview of its marvels have already commented that it easily surpasses all and any effort ever seen on the streets of Slagway. Indeed, I exaggerate not one whit when I say that it is a splendour hitherto unseen – and I emphasise *unseen* – anywhere in the whole of the western world."

Maximus pauses, leans forward at the rostrum and so looks into the crowd that each and every listener believes that he or she is the particular one upon whom the FART is gazing. "But, my dear friends, that said, nothing is anything until it meets with the approval of the most discerning: for you, the citizens of Slagway, and those of you who have come here from other towns and cities – yea, from other countries, even – to view this day's parade, are unquestionably the most discerning of all judges."

He eases back from the rostrum a little, a half glance to one side, impeccable in his timing, then leans in towards the mic again. "People of Slagway, I give you the Fresh Air Theme."

An explosion, as though of thunder, and a gushing cloud of smoke that is a mixture of pink and purple hues, obscures all on the platform from the gaze of those assembled. Even Maximus, titan of all situations, is occluded from their view. Then, in the most spectacular of fashions, from amidst the murky depths of smoky cloud, emerges a string of dancers, half-naked and demonic in

appearance, their faces smeared with lines of black and
reddish paints, their hair so wild and vivid of colour that
even thoughts of such follicular arrangement have never
previously entered the mind of man or beast. The dancers
weave mesmeric lines of passage through the gathering,
enchanting, entrancing, enhancing every sense of
expectation with which the loyal onlookers have come on
this day of days in their otherwise quite ordinary lives.

Martineen turns in towards a shopfront on the north
end of the Square, pulls forward the hood in which his
head had earlier been deeply embedded and furtively
invites his mobile phone to join him in seclusion. "Hello,
Stepheneen, hello, dis is Martineen. Are ya dare?"

On the opposite side of the Square, Stepheneen, busily
struggling to hear above the din, also now turns in towards
the shopfront of an establishment – a ladies' lingerie
boutique – to which he has most puritanically had his back
turned until now.

"Martineen, Martineen, is it yarself dat's in it?"

"For Jaysus sake, what are ya on about? Haven't I just
feckinwell told ya it's me? D'ya tink I'm talkin' ta meself or
what?"

"What?"

Suddenly, a second explosion at the top end of the
Square puts an end to conversation between the would-be
topplers of the world of shaperdom and a second surge of
dancers runs from behind the platform and, as had their
predecessors done before them, weave amongst the crowd.
The smoke around the platform area has cleared for now
and the dignitaries are seen to laugh and applaud, showing
gleeful approval of all that is happening below. Another

gushing emission of multicoloured smoke, then obfuscation becomes the order of the moment again.

"Mawrvellous, mawrvellous," Maximus comments to the mayor, then both show signs of choking on the density of the smoke which has begun to flirt with their olfactory orifices.

"Hello, hello, are ya still dare, Stepheneen, are ya?" shouts Martineen above the noise, and then he takes the mobile phone and taps it hard against the shopfront window, causing the alarm of the building in question to activate itself. In relative terms, the whirring of the alarm makes little difference to the noise level in general, but Martineen's proximity to the establishment makes it considerably more difficult for him to hear whether or not Stepheneen is at the other end of the line.

"Ah, shite," he says, in frustration, and surrenders his phone to the junk heap by venomously smashing it down on the head of one of the passing dancers, sending various minutiae of technological endeavour flying in all directions.

And now a third explosion, followed by yet another smoke emission, and a throne most splendid, painted in gold and silver and mounted on a platform, is wheeled into view, occasioning gasps of wonderment and spontaneous applause from all who witness its emergence. Atop of the throne sits none other than good ould get-in-on-the-act-and-be-sure-to-be-seen Secundus, his head bedecked in what appears to be a mixture of slimy kelp and rejected stringy bits from some slurry pit that has been specially developed somewhere to the leeward side of Slagway.

Secundus stands now, bollock-naked, bar the skimpy loincloth which he wears and on the design and making of

which no less than eight members of his dutiful crew have
spent the winter long.

"Arraghhh," he bellows threateningly at the crowd,
causing them, at first, to back away in unison and then to
burst into applause in appreciation of his innovative and
artistic utterance. Such talent, they think. It is but the first
of many such 'Arraghhhs' he will issue throughout the
course of the parade, each bellowed with an uncannily
studied sameness. This is Art, they think to themselves; this
is real and living Art. Our friend, the Fly, never one to
figure too overtly where shaperdom is known to strut its
stuff, has ensconced himself in the middle of the weird
assemblage of weed and weed-upon material on Secundus'
head. He is surveyor of all and, indeed, from his perch, he
has already spotted Martineen and Stepheneen on their
respective sides of the crowd.

"And now the *pièce de résistance*," announces Maximus,
having stepped forward to the mic to draw the crowd's
attention to the emergence of those who follow the
arraghhhing Secundus' throne, "the Fresh Air Theme."
Now the onlookers' attention is drawn to the two lines of
Secundus' devotees who walk behind the wheeled throne,
displaying the Fresh Air Theme for all to see, or even
displaying it for all not to see. Each of these artistically
holds one of the aforementioned poles of Sheffield steel
upright as he moves and, lest any in the gathering be in
doubt as to what it is that he or she is supposed to see,
Maximus, still at the mic, again contributes to their
understanding saying: "Look at all that ma*w*rvellous Fresh
Air hanging on those splendidly crafted poles. Bubbles and
bubbles of the most ma*w*rvellous fresh air."

Maximus' utterance and the crowd's awareness of his supreme appreciation of what is Art immediately prompts them to believe that so sophisticated is this display which parades itself before them that they simply have not yet aspired to that point in their own appreciation where they can fully understand the aesthetic import of what it is that is artistically passing before their eyes. Of course, that's it: it is the ultimate in artistic sophistication – the fresh air. How brilliant that Secundus and his team could so construct it that, just as fresh air has always been, this which is on display today is equally invisible. A feat supreme, indeed.

"Yes, yes!" one shitehawk in the crowd exclaims, and then begins to applaud in approval of the wonderful display. There is a contagion in his words that causes others to do likewise and, in no time at all, every member in the gathering (with the notable exception of your pals and mine, i.e. Martineen and Stepheneen) afford an unprecedented ovation to the creators of the ultimate in Art.

"Fresh Air, Fresh Air, Fresh Air, Fresh Air," the crowd chants, each word couplet being shouted louder than that which has preceded it.

On hearing the crowd's enthusiasm for what it is they see/don't see, Secundus turns back to look at Maximus and the latter winks knowingly at his second-in-command. Only the Fly is privy to this deed and, with the sole exception of the two saboteurs in the crowd, only he can see through the wool which has been visited upon the eyes of all below. Secundus then shifts his gaze to meet the eye of Administratus, who now stands alongside Maximus on the platform. The best that Y-J can do is force the suggestion of a smile, which does not even realise a parting of his lips. In his mind, he knows that the outstanding ovation given to Secundus' efforts only serves to strengthen the clod-hopper's hold on the number two position. How he detests this day each year, and yet he comes religiously, year in year out, always in the hope that some day, somehow, Secundus will finally come a cropper.

"Arraghhh," the now ebullient Shaperus Secundus roars and then, with great gusto, he juts his right arm forward pointing to the route the parade will take. "To Hops Street, Arraghhh," he bellows, then sits back on his throne.

Now Martineen and Stepheneen move with great alacrity, skilfully weaving through the crowd and making their way towards the top of Hops Street. They know their people are strategically dotted on the pavements on either side of the route, armed as are their leaders, and, when they see their elders move along the route, they too will abandon their positions and follow to that point in the road that is traditionally known as The Great Fork. As the Rabble-Moracennan number swells in close pursuit of the parade, a subtle touching of a forefinger against the side of the nose serves as signal to their remaining members to leave the pavements also.

"Arraghhh," yells the bould Secundus aloft upon his throne, oblivious to the world that, by now, most of those in the pursuing entourage are more his enemies than his friends. The Fly, still prettily perched upon the barker's head, has taken stock of the attendant Rabble-Moracennans and, if ever there has been a moment when he has had occasion to thank his ancestry for the gift of flight, it is unquestionably now.

"Arrraghhh, arrraghhh-arrraghhh." Secundus' triple delivery is evoked by the sight of the fast-approaching Great Fork. He knows of old that, as the display takes the right-hand thoroughfare at the fork in the road, sight of the parade will soon be lost to those already passed and, somehow, it seems to him that these last few growls, issued exclusively for their benefit, will be forever treasured by them. He stands to one side of the throne's platform to wave goodbye to those who will be left behind when, suddenly, a jerk of the wheeled vehicle throws him back into the seat and causes him to bang his head against one of the wooden orbs mounted on the armrests of the throne.

The jerk – that *of* the throne, rather than that *on* the throne – has been no accident. It has been the result of a well co-ordinated shove by the Rabble-Moracennans and suddenly the throne is being directed down along Sigh Street, rather than the planned route across the bridge and into Modinick Street. Those dancers ahead of the throne have proceeded merrily along the pre-planned itinerary, oblivious to what has happened behind them, while those behind the golden seat, carriers of the weighty Fresh Air display, follow the throne in its misdirection.

Throne, entourage and trailing parade of the Fresh Air Theme hurtle downhill through the city's Latin Quarter and, as they do so, the Rabble-Moracennans unveil their weapons and begin to jab at the invisibility that is hoisted on the shapers' poles of Sheffield steel. The shapers, realising what is happening, cannot allow it to be seen by the Slagway public that they are mere pretenders (to the throne?) and at least have the savvy to know that if a bubble of air is so pricked and prodded, there will be, if not a veritable explosion, then at least the sound of hissing as the air escapes. So, knowing what it is that must be done in the name of saving face, they begin to hiss. And the more they hiss, the more the Rabble-Moracennans prod and prick, and the more the latter prod and prick, then the more again the former hiss.

Hiss – prod, *hiss* – prick, *hiss* – prod-prod, *hiss* – prick-prick, *hiss-hiss-hiss* – prickidy-prick-prod-prod, *hissidy-hiss-hissidy-hiss* – prickidy-prickidy-prod-prick-prick.

"Oh, my God! Oh, my God!" exclaims Secundus, as he regains his footing on the lofted throne. He looks ahead of him and, in the distance, sees the harbour wall and, on the pier, thousands of the city's faithful, cheering gleefully at what is, they think, most certainly the most daring of any of the parades that they have witnessed. The sudden and unannounced re-altering of a route shows real initiative, as far as the onlookers are concerned. Secundus is despairing, but not yet so desperately that he will not contribute to an attempted saving of face.

"Arraghhh – *hiss-hiss*," he cries. And now the crowd on the dockside cheer even more.

"Arraghh – *hiss-fucking-hiss-fucking-hiss-hiss-hiss*," he cries now, that little bit more desperate than heretofore. The tumult think the expletive a sign of even greater enthusiasm on Secundus' part and they cheer all the louder. Secundus now, eyes bulging so much at the prospect of a dip in Slagway Bay that their staying in their sockets defies all hitherto known laws of stress and gravity. Anticipating the worst, he summons shapers one and all to the call with a fear-filled cry of "All hands on deck for the cause of

Shaperdom – *hiss-hiss*."

Out of anywhere and everywhere, the shapers of Slagway rally to the call and latch themselves fast, like veritable noras (old Slagway literary word for barnacles), onto the hurtling wheel-mounted throne, little realising that their extra weight, rather than slowing its passage to the sea, will, in fact, have quite the opposite effect. All now are hurtling towards the water at a rate previously unknown to man. The crowd below has parted, appreciating in no small way what they think to be the unsparing efforts of every Slagway shaper to provide for them a spectacle unrivalled by any parade before or after.

Just as the very last of all available shapers latches on to the trundling mass of fresh air, Secundus emits the final of his cries, this time displaying an element of creativity in his wording for which he has never before been known:

"Arriddy-aghh-fucking-aghhhhhhhhhhh," he cries, and then his bulging eyes focus despairingly on the all-too-lowly-set metal retaining bar on the edge of the harbour wall. The crowd, just lately realising that the impetus with which the whole shabang is hurtling towards them is not in keeping with the notion of stopping, quickly parts, allowing the lower part of the wheeled platform to make maximum impact with the retaining bar. All aboard – Secundus, throne and all – are jettisoned in a most unship-shaperly fashion out into the bay, so far out, indeed, that their point of landing – much like, dare one say it, the fresh air – is invisible to all who now gather again on the dockside.

For several seconds, both throne and shapers are strewn like jetsam across the mouth of the bay. A bobbing and a weaving, in perfect keeping with the water's undulation, is seen on the surface, then suddenly, all disappears below. Those gathered on the quayside still look on, amazed, aghast, agog at all that they have witnessed. Then Neptune, in his vengeance, emits one unmerciful and gynormous belch, violently spewing all that he has swallowed skywards once again, and waits for its return into the bowels of deepest darkness.

14

There'll be Fun and Laughter and Peace Ever Rafter ...

A sad and wailing cry creeps in off the bay and wends a lonely course throughout Slagway's abandoned streets. It is several years since anything approaching artistic mention in any shaper form has been overtly heard in these environs. Young children in the city have only ever heard accidental allusion to such animals as shapers – that when their parents or, more likely still, their grandparents, in moments of laxness have let the half-reference slip as an ellipsis from their lips. Elliptical lip slippage of such a kind has become a major offence in the town of Slagway, but, most often, such has happened within the dwellings of such utterers and has, for the most part, gone unreported. Even history texts used in schools inside the city walls are, by decree of the Right Honorable Mayor Martineen the Liberator, bereft of description of not just the phenomenon that once was known as shaper, but of the very mention of the word itself.

It is many years since the ill-reputed Fresh Air Theme saw shaperdom ingloriously on its way to the Fluffy By and By. All aboard for Shapers' Paradise! And so it is that, somewhere above, Secundus and his mates are playing their tuneless airs on stringless harps and designing the invisible to their hearts' content.

Of their number, all but three managed to catch the last throne to Paradise – the only throne to Paradise – and, despite the years of blight that they inflicted on the innocent of Slagway, they are, nonetheless, surely deserving of reference here: Administratus, Y-J, call him what you will, has since taken permanently to the bed, a faded mirror clutched in one hand and that still unread abbreviated version of *Ulysses* in the other. That pimple of his is growing daily and it is his fervent hope that, someday soon, it will so augment itself that it will violently explode, the force thereby occasioned propelling him skywards and beyond. And there he will, at last, join his fellow-shapers.

As for Maximus, the FART supreme: last reports have been that he has headed for the lesser fishing town of Tuna, south of Slagway, where mention of the Arts has rarely, if at all, been heard. There have been mootings that he has been seen working nets or, as others far more practised in the pointed prickly art of needlecraft might put it, 'networking'.

And, alas, Poetica. Poor Poetryless Poetica: she who would have been, should have been, but alas, couldn't be what she had most desired. That wailing cry of earlier allusion, the strains of which creep in off the bay, is the lonesome keen of none other than the hapless scribe. Martineen, just like herself, had proven two-faced and, once the world of shaperdom had been overthrown, he had little time for she with whom he (and, let's face it, everybody else) had had his way. Yet another of his decrees has seen to her banishment to the sea. A vessel, imaginatively christened RAFT, was specially constructed at the city's expense and, one wet and windy morning, a gathering of the city's councillors ushered it seawards from the harbour wall. Amongst those assembled at the dockside was Martineen himself, and he, most curiously, has more recently announced that, when finally the elements come to claim its occupants for their own and the vessel RAFT is swept back in to shore, he, being first citizen of the city, will have automatic right to possession of same as a final reminder of the one-time evil that was shaperdom.

On board the said RAFT is our Poetica, a voracious and overgrown twin sucking ravenously at each breast and the would-be essentials of her life – a pen and paper – dangling from her fingertips, as her babes hang out of her. It is only our friend, the Fly, who knows of the creative juices that have been flowing from her since the time of her expulsion. His hearing, more acutely honed than that of the mere mortal, has been of great assistance to him in identifying the tones of her wailing cry for what it really is. Yes, at last, she has hit the jackpot and come up with a verse of true originality. The winged polyglot himself has translated it and has deemed it worthy of attention by seafarers of every nationality:

> *Óró om dáibhín ga mánsh ra na cguan,*
> *Ó-óró om rruchaichín-ó,*
> *Rrattaigí, rrattaigí, rrattaigí og uban,*
> *Ó-óró om dáibhín.*

All of which the phantom flier has unerringly interpreted as meaning:

> *O-row my boateen out there in the bay,*
> *O-row my boateen-o;*
> *Row ye-e, row ye-e, row ye away,*
> *O-o-row my boateen.*

'Bejay, da very bessht a' pottery, indeed,' as the departed Secundus might, would, but, alas now, can no longer say.

And finally, of course, our aforementioned friend, the Fly, who, with his philosophy of '*Neither a Shaper nor a Rabble-Moracennan be*', has remained marvellously and independently unattached throughout.

His place of greatest habitude these times has become the City Council chambers, where he has made a snug and quiet nest for himself atop of the ceramic city crest, overlooking Mayor Martineen the Liberator's seat of power. Lately, his awareness of his role and calling as deadly stinger of all and anything that may need a little stinging has been heightened once again, as, from his perch on high, he has noticed Martineen's doodling on his inkpad has, in the main, ominously featured the various configural arrangements of that word RAFT ...

ECSTASY
and other stories
by
Ré Ó Laighléis
(ISBN 0-9532777-9-8)

This acclaimed collection looks at the rise, the fall and the versatility of the human spirit, touching, as it does, on almost every aspect of human trial and existence. Though unflinchingly hard-hitting, it is utterly compelling and written with great insight and sensitivity. Ó Laighléis' greatest gift is that he is a masterful story-teller.

"This combination of style and tone provides a maturity which rarely characterises writing targeted mainly at a teenage readership ... It deserves the widest possible audience."
Robert Dunbar, *The Irish Times*

"Always there is an appropriate honed-down style that presents the narratives in crystal clear detail ... Not just a book for teenagers, but for everyone who appreciates first-class writing."
Tony Hickey, *Village*

"Ó Laighléis is not one for the soft option. He deals unflinchingly with major social issues that affect all our lives and deals with them with profound insight and intelligence ... It is Ó Laighléis' creative imagination that gives the collection its undeniable power. The economy of his prose allows for no authorial moralising." **Books Ireland**

*"*Ecstasy and other stories *is brilliantly written and an eye-opener for us all as to what could happen if life takes that one wrong turn. Ré Ó Laighléis is a master of his craft."*
Geraldine Molloy, *The Big Issues*

*"*Ecstasy *is evocative of the filmography of Ken Loach, and its minimalistic story-telling, with its sparse and essential style, constitutes an extraordinarily expressive force."*
Mondadori, Milan, Italy (publishers)

"The short stories of Ecstasy *... take us, in the Irish context, into new thematic territories and, more importantly, pay their characters (and, by extension, their readers) the compliment of allowing them to live with the consequences of their own choices: complex circumstances are always seen to defy easy outcomes."*
Books, *The Irish Times Weekend Supplement*

HOOKED
by
Ré Ó Laighléis
(ISBN 0-9532777-1-2)

Ó Laighléis' highly acclaimed novel tells the horrific and gruelling tale of teenager Alan's slide into the world of drug addiction and his involvement with its murky and danger-filled underworld. Equally importantly, *Hooked* also relates the parents' story: Sandra's world is thrown into turmoil, first by the realisation that her 17-year-old son is in the throes of heroin addiction and then by the discovery of her husband's infidelity. There are no ribbons wrapped around the story here – it is hard, factual and written with sensitivity and skill.

"It is a riveting story based on every parent's nightmare."
Lorna Siggins, *The Irish Times*

"Ó Laighléis deftly favours creating a dark side of urban life over sledge-hammering the reader with 'Just Say No' messages; the horrors of heroin addiction are revealed within the story itself and, thankfully, the author avoids any preachy commentary." **Educationmatters**

"Hooked *inhabits the world of well-off middle-class Dublin ... with all its urban angst, moral decay, drug addiction, loneliness and teen attitudes and problems."*
Patrick Brennan, *Irish Independent*

"Ré Ó Laighléis speaks the language of those for whom Hooked *will strike a familiar chord. If it makes people stop and think – as it undoubtedly will – it will have achieved more than all the anti-drug promotional campaigns we could ever begin to create."*
News Focus, *The Mayo News*

"Ó Laighléis deftly walks that path between the fields of teenage and adult literature, resulting in a book that will have wide appeal for both young and older readers." **Paddy Kehoe, *RTÉ Guide***

"The book pulls no punches and there are no happy endings."
Colin Kerr, *News of the World*

ALSO AVAILABLE FROM MÓINÍN

TERROR ON THE BURREN
by
Ré Ó Laighléis
(ISBN 0-9532777-0-4)

This multiple award-winning and critically acclaimed novel is a superlative mix of the supernatural and the real. Set against the archaeological and geological richness of the Burren landscape in Ireland's County Clare, the author weaves a mesmeric and multi-layered tale of barbarity and beauty, of the imaginative and intrigue, of good and evil.

"Measured, even against his own already high standards, Ré Ó Laighléis has given us an exceptional work of beauty and terror here. This, quite simply, stands apart." **C. J. Haughey, former Taoiseach**

"Another example of Ó Laighléis' shining creations ... Undoubtedly, Ó Laighléis is a gifted writer and we wait with hungry curiosity to see what he will come up with next."
Tom Widger, *The Sunday Tribune*

"You'll never look at the Burren in the same way after you read this tale ... Anyone even slightly intrigued by alternatives to the 20th century's blue-print for living will find this account of life in 200 BC enchanting ... The whole saga unfolds within a slim 114 pages, with the mystical beauty of the Burren permeating every page."
Sharon Diviney, *Ireland on Sunday*

"This is an unusual work of rich and cinematographic prose, a work of excellence in the fantasy genre and one which bears the scope of The Mists of Avalon." **Gabriel Rosenstock, Writer**

"Though ostensibly set on the Burren in the period of prehistory, Ó Laighléis' horrific story of destruction is inextricably connected to more recent murky happenings."
**Prof. Mícheál Mac Craith,
National University of Ireland, Galway**

"A brilliant and fascinating read, which will hold you enthralled to the very end." **Geraldine Molloy, *The Big Issues***

"This is epic story-telling at its very best." **Tony Hickey, *Village***

HEART OF BURREN STONE
A collection of short stories
by
Ré Ó Laighléis
(ISBN 0-9532777-2-0)

National and international award-winning author Ré Ó Laighléis gives us a collection that is disturbingly provocative, yet permeated throughout by a humane and perceptive sensitivity. His stories alternate between the serious and witty. Set against both urban and rural backgrounds, these stories range in location from England to the United States and from France to Ireland North and South, with a concentration on the Burren.

Ó Laighléis is equally adept whether handling the loss of childhood innocence in cosmopolitan Dublin or remotest rural Ireland, the depravity that, at times, replaces such innocence in adult years, or the twists in life that determine happiness and misery. His characters bear all the frailty and vulnerability that epitomise the difficulty of survival in contemporary society.

Whether the tragicomedy of two nine-year-olds arguing their political corners on the North of Ireland's Garvaghy Road, the conniving roguery of a Burren publisher or the pain-filled dilemma of a dying cancer patient in a Boston hospital appealing to be assisted on his way – there is an unnerving universality to Ó Laighléis' writing.

BATTLE FOR THE BURREN

Sequel to **Terror on the Burren**
by
Ré Ó Laighléis

It is 1317 AD, some 1,500 years since the visionary Sobharthan fought her epic battle against evil on the shores of Loch Reasc. Though long since dead, her spirit is embodied in the old blind monk, Benignus, who, like her, has been both blessed and cursed with the gift of vision. He is an elder of the community of Cistercians who occupy the monastery at Corcomroe on the Burren's beautiful, yet unforgiving foothills.

Set against the great wars of the divided factions of the Clan O'Brien, the power of evil has found a willing home in the heart and soul of the dark and sinister Feardorcha, a lieutenant in the forces of Prince Donncha O'Brien. The opposing forces of Donncha and his cousin, Turlough, are making for the holy place at Corcomroe, where, once and for all, the bloodiest of battles will be fought to determine supremacy within the Clan O'Brien. And bloody it will be, and such will be the ensuing slaughter that devastation of its kind will be unprecedented.

This is the backdrop against which young Iarla O'Brien, son of Turlough, conducts his secretive and passion-filled relationship with Sorcha, daughter of Mahon, one of Prince Donncha's most ardent and loyal supporters. Though filled with love and hope for a future together, the young lovers are all too aware of the divisions between their families and of the dangers that lie ahead. Their fates are outside of them and will ultimately be determined by the powers of Good and Evil. An epic tale of love, of fear, of darkness.